TRUE STARS COLLIDE

CLAIRE MARTI

True Stars Collide

Copyright © 2023 by Claire Marti

ISBN: eBook 979-8-9884416-6-3

ISBN: Paperback 979-8-9884416-5-6

Published By: Claire Marti

Editor: Lindsey Faber

Proofreader: Shasta Shaefer

Cover Design: Sarah Paige, The Book Cover Boutique

❀ Created with Vellum

For my favorite misunderstood rock stars...

CHAPTER 1

Zoe crooned the last few words of one of the most famous rock ballads of all time. She set the microphone into the cradle, stepped back, and squeezed her eyes closed. The room fell silent, each member of Black Velvet Machine quiet. One person started clapping and another joined in. One by one, they filled the studio audition space with applause.

She exhaled and opened her eyes. Krissy, her best friend and agent, stood across the room, wearing an enormous grin, her dark eyes sparkling with joy.

"That was bloody brilliant, Zoe. The best we've heard, isn't that right, boys?" The bright blue eyes of Black Velvet Machine's manager, Ian Sheldon, blazed with pure calculation.

Cautious joy battled with crushing anxiety in her chest. Could this really be happening? Would her dream of finally singing for an alt-rock band finally be coming true? No more harmonizing with the pop group she'd been forced to perform with ever again.

"Thank you. The song is so beautiful, it's an honor to sing

it." No pressure––the ex-lead singer whose shoes she longed to fill had written it.

"Yeah, the ballad worked. What I can't see working is you pulling the range on the anthems and heavier songs. How are you going to pull off Austin Michaels' signature howl?" Liam Jones, legendary lead guitarist, smirked at her from across the stage.

The infamous blond rocker hadn't said a word to her––not even hello––when she'd arrived. Nope, he'd flashed a scathing glance at her, his eyes frozen chips of bottle green glass, his upper lip curled in a sneer worthy of Billy Idol. He was renowned for his signature open chord progression style, earning comparisons to Slash and Jimi Hendrix. But while his musical genius was world-renowned, his surly attitude and sexual escapades were notorious.

"Liam," André, the drummer who looked more like an NFL Linebacker than a musician, growled. "Shut it, man."

Nobody else uttered a word.

Her battle.

Her lifelong dream.

So "Love 'em and Leave 'em Liam" didn't think she could hit those high notes? Accustomed to being underestimated, Zoe merely flashed a smile at him. Time to wipe that smug smile off his too-handsome face.

"I'll take that as a compliment and a challenge. Nobody can match Austin Michaels and I'm not gonna try. But I think you'll be happy with the Zoe Hastings version." The pompous British prick would eat his words and fall to his knees once she was done.

Because she'd prepared the band's top ten hits before today's audition. Besides, she'd been a fan for years, so singing with the band instead of in the shower was a dream come true.

"Did you prep *Lightning Strikes*?" Ben, the soft-spoken bass guitarist sporting a leather vest, asked.

"Ready when you are." Adrenaline coursed through her veins. Singing for Black Velvet Machine was her ultimate gig. Failure wasn't an option.

Liam grunted and muttered something under his breath, but kept his eyes trained on his Gibson. No time to deal with his six foot something of bad attitude right now. She'd survived singing in a five-girl pop band––she could handle anything.

André began the intro to *Lightning Strikes*, a loud thundering tempo and Ben and Liam joined in, setting her up. The song built gradually before exploding into fast, furious vocals and a pumping beat.

Now or never, Zoe. The music flooded her being, the seductive pulsing rhythm filling her. She flipped her hair over her shoulder, grabbed the mike, and let loose. She stalked around the stage, allowing the music to overtake her. She nailed every high note—hell, she nailed the entire song. Four minutes later, she dropped to her knees, and dropped the mic.

If that performance didn't earn her the job, it wasn't because she hadn't rocked it. Her breath came in rapid bursts and her heart knocked against her ribs. She wasn't tired, she was exhilarated. For years, she'd been obliged to sing the way others demanded. Today was about unleashing her authentic voice.

Ben stepped over and offered her a hand. "As far as I'm concerned, you're in."

"Thank you." She accepted his assistance, although Ben wasn't much bigger than she was, and she was 5'1. Well, without her four-inch boots anyway.

Krissy was fist-pumping in the air, Ian was nodding and rubbing the scruff on his jaw.

Liam stared at her with narrowed eyes, his chiseled lips pressed into a tight line. "Color me impressed. Nice range."

Because of course he hadn't bothered to listen to her demo tape. If he had, he wouldn't have been so shocked. Or maybe he'd have assumed she'd auto-tuned the crap out of it. Either way, she'd take the praise, no matter how grudgingly he offered it. No need to antagonize him nor poke at the hefty chip on his shoulder. They didn't need to become friends, but some form of respect would be nice.

"I'm with Ben. Didn't think a chick lead singer would work for us. You're dead on that nobody can sing like Austin, but that's the past. Fans clamor for Austin and for Tommy. But they're both gone. I'm the drummer now. I think you'll help us bring Black Velvet Machine back, version 2.0. Liam?" André's smooth baritone held conviction.

Liam scrubbed his hands through his shoulder length mess of blond curls. "Yeah, the voice and the performance work. But how many of our fans are going to buy into a pop princess as our front-person? I mean, for fuck's sake, just a couple years ago, she fronted the Baby Dolls, they catered to little girls."

Zoe's lips parted but no words emerged. She'd had valid reasons for signing with the soul-sucking ensemble. After finally escaping the draconian contract, she'd spent the last two years laying low, penning new songs––songs true to her voice. But he wasn't wrong––her image needed re-vamping.

So, she'd dyed her chestnut hair jet-black, finally sported her full sleeve tattoo the record company had forbidden, and wore enough black eyeliner to impress Alice Cooper. Right now she wore low-slung red leather pants and a ripped white tank top.

Not exactly Baby Dolls attire.

Krissy clapped her hands together. "Let's put the image

issues on hold for a minute. If we've got a plan for that, are you guys unanimous in wanting Zoe?"

"Hell yeah. We're ready to get this album recorded. The songs are ready, we've already laid down some of the tracks. Time to tour again. It's been way too long." Ben waved his long-neck beer bottle and took a swig.

"Like I said, yeah," André smacked the cymbals for emphasis.

"Liam? If I can guarantee we've got not just Zoe's image problem covered but also a plan to diffuse the issues from the interview you gave claiming Austin was returning, you in?" Ian quirked a brow.

"Yeah, dude, the fans are still pissed at that bait and switch." Ben shoved back floppy ginger hair from his forehead.

Liam held up a hand. "Mate, I took a gamble."

A gamble? Zoe bit the inside of her cheek. Last month, a big news story dropped that Austin Michaels was returning to the band after leaving three years ago when their drummer, Tommy Ash, had overdosed. In fact, Austin had zero plans to return, and the fans had been outraged.

"Liam," the band's general manager snapped.

"Fine, yeah. If you've got some magic strategy, I think she's worth at least a trial run for this album."

Asshole. Of course he couldn't just say yes. Although now wasn't the time or place to call him on it. She knew how to play the game. Winning did not involve arguing with the guy in charge of her destiny.

Because if Liam said no, the band would keep looking. He was the heart and soul of the group and had the final word. She'd bide her time. Once she was in, she and Mr. Bad Attitude would have a little chat.

"Awesome. Liam and Zoe, let's meet at my office in an hour. We'll share the plan because you're both involved. We'll get it sorted this afternoon and fast-track recording the new album and cementing the tour schedule. Deal?" Ian was all business.

"Perfect. I'll see you there." Joy filled Zoe's heart. Finally, at the ripe old age of 27, she was going to perform on her terms. No more hiding herself behind a fake image.

How outrageous could the PR plan be?

CHAPTER 2

*L*iam parked, ripped off his helmet, and stepped off his prized Harley. He stared up at the neon green monstrosity that housed the band's general manager's office. Whoever had designed that shit should be drawn and quartered. Call him old-school but he hated the glass and concrete jungle that made up Los Angeles.

He strode to the entrance and through the glass and chrome fun-house lobby to the elevator. At least Ian had the fucking top floor. The elevator doors slid open, and he stepped inside. And lo and behold, Zoe "Pop Princess" Hastings stood in the corner, her tawny cat eyes wide.

The doors closed silently behind him. Four floors alone together until they met with the team. Great. He nodded at her, not keen on starting a conversation. Yeah, he knew he'd been a dick, but why try to hide his true colors?

"Hi Liam," she said in her sexy as hell voice.

"Hey." He leaned against the elevator wall and crossed his arms over his chest.

She brushed a strand of long ebony hair off her truly spectacular face. She wasn't classically pretty, but you couldn't take your eyes off her. From those huge tip-tilted golden eyes, high cheekbones, rosebud lips, down to her small pointed chin, she was arresting. Interesting. Compelling. He'd seen photos of her on tons of magazine covers in the past.

Then, she'd had shiny, bouncy Victoria's Secret hair and polished perfect make-up. Like every other plastic looking Influencer chick out there. Yeah, the messy black hair, heavy eyeliner, and full sleeve tattoo did make her look more Blondie than Britney.

But an incredible voice and looks weren't enough to erase her past.

Even with the dangerous curves she sported on her petite frame. Yeah, he'd noticed her ass in the supple red leather. Hell, a dead man would have noticed the way her tiny waist curved into that rounded perfection.

Tension simmered in the elevator, and he caught a hint of her perfume, something rich and spicy, jasmine maybe? He held his breath.

"So, I wonder what the PR team has planned to toughen me up? Give me a motorcycle? Have me trashing hotel rooms or chugging Wild Turkey for breakfast?" Her unpainted mouth quirked up at one corner.

He laughed. "Definitely the bourbon, as long as you drink out of the bottle, Jim Morrison style." So she had a sense of humor. He could work with that.

"Oh yeah, I can channel Mr. Mojo Rising for sure. I'm willing to do whatever it takes to shed the teeny bopper image, so they can do their worst. My public image was never me."

Huh, she seemed eager to convey that point. He'd wait and see. But he couldn't deny she could belt it out. Wondered why the hell she hadn't been in real music until now.

The elevator bell dinged and the doors parted, opening

into the plush penthouse offices. A pretty, young receptionist beamed at him and batted her cartoon eyelashes. Yawn. "Mr. Jones, they're waiting for you both in the West conference room."

He turned to Zoe. "Follow me."

"Are they always like that with you?" She arched one ebony eyebrow and fell into step beside him.

He shrugged. "You know the gig, celebrities are fair game, at least when they're on top."

She rolled her eyes. "Yeah, I used to get mobbed by sixth grade girls. That receptionist was probably one of them a few years ago."

They traversed a long hallway and reached the glass-walled conference room, where their managers and PR team gathered at one end of a Titanic-sized table. Frustration flared down his spine—everything in this business except for the writing, playing, and performing of music—ticked him off. What had these people looking so smug? Yeah, he wasn't going to like it.

Zoe opened the door before he had a chance, and he followed her inside.

"Perfect, the two of you already hanging out together." One of the PR suits smirked.

Krissy rose and smiled brightly. "We're really excited, guys. Have a seat so we can run through this and get started."

Zoe's eyes went wide, and her cheeks paled.

What did she know that he didn't?

Not like he had a choice. He'd majorly fucked up by telling all the major entertainment outlets Austin was returning to the band when he knew it was bullshit. But he'd figured his former bandmate and friend would cave to the pressure.

And he'd been dead fucking wrong.

The blow back had been fierce. After three years, the fans

were impatient and had moved on to the latest new band. If Black Velvet Machine stood a chance of a come-back, it had to happen before time ran out.

So whatever the suits had up their sleeves? He'd have to play along with it because he bore the brunt of the mistake. He paid his debts.

Zoe crossed the room and sat beside her agent. So much for them presenting a united front. He flopped down next to his manager, facing her and the floor-to-ceiling windows letting in the unrelenting blue sky and sunshine. Sometimes he missed the gray skies of the U.K.--more suited to his moods.

"What's the magic plan?" Zoe folded her slender hands together and rested them on the charcoal granite table.

Krissy blew out a breath. "Ian, you want to present it or should I?"

Ian gestured with one hand. "Take it away."

"Hear me out before you say a word." Zoe's agent narrowed her eyes at him.

He shrugged a shoulder and Zoe gave a sharp nod.

"We've brainstormed, and agree we need something dramatic, over-the-top, exciting, and fast. This plan is the best way to integrate Zoe and stir up so much attention that the fans will forget about the false tease of Austin's return.

"Zoe needs to seem wild and unpredictable. Think total opposite of her Baby Dolls girly image. You two will go to Vegas and party all over town. We'll tip off the press, who will photograph you together, making out, drinking, being outrageous."

"Outrageous in Vegas?" Zoe asked. "Isn't everyone?"

Krissy held up a finger. "Shh, I'm not done. Then, you two will go to City Hall and pick up a marriage license, where some paparazzi will conveniently spot you. Then, your driver will take you through The Little White Wedding Chapel where you'll get married--"

Liam surged to his feet. "You're out of your fucking mind if you think I'm getting married."

"Sit. Your ass. Down." Ian bit out the words.

He dropped into the stiff leather chair, his fingers curling around the chrome armrests. No fucking way. He'd always been single and liked it that way.

Zoe's expression was blank.

Zoe's agent continued as if he hadn't spoken. "You will get married and return to your honeymoon suite at the Virgin Hotel. From that moment forward, in public, you two are mad for each other. PDA everywhere. Never seen alone. Then, two nights later, Black Velvet Machine will play a surprise exclusive show at The Theater at Virgin Hotel. Bam--the band will officially be back. You two will be seen as the faces of the band. Zoe and Liam. Liam and Zoe.

"Once you return to California, you'll live together at Liam's place in Santa Barbara. The band will lay down all the tracks for the new album in Liam's recording studio. You'll kick off with the already scheduled 30 date/21 city North American Tour in the end of September. Now you can ask your questions."

Liam shoved away from the table and stalked to the windows. "A marriage to save the band? That's the dumbest idea I've ever heard."

"C'mon, Liam. You know there are probably more fake relationships than real ones in Hollywood. It works," Ian said.

"Why me? My reputation works. Why not Ben? He's the other original member." He struggled to regulate the red hazing his vision.

"You're the leader of the band, not Ben, and you know it. You fucked things up. You need to fix it. Period."

Liam turned and fixed his gaze on Zoe, who sat frozen in place. "There's got to be some other way. What the hell would you do if we'd chosen a guy? Would I have had to marry him?"

Krissy snorted. "That point is moot. If you care so much about resurrecting Black Velvet Machine to its former glory, do it. Ian confirmed you and Zoe are both single."

Irritated that Zoe hadn't made a peep, he pointed at her. "Did you know about this?"

Zoe smoothed her wild tangle of ebony hair away from her face and gazed up at him, her whiskey-colored eyes unreadable. "No, I did not know about this."

"That's all you're going to say? You're okay with this?" He gritted his teeth.

"I don't want to marry you any more than you want to marry me. But this kind of thing works. I want the band to be a success and I'm willing to do whatever it takes, even if that means acting like we..." She trailed off, her gaze dropping to her clasped hands.

"Well, you're used to pretending, right? You're just exchanging one bullshit image for another."

Her nostrils flared and her lips tightened. "Grow up, we're in show business. Everyone has a public persona. Although having an image for the public and faking a marriage aren't exactly the same. But at the end of the day, I'll be singing rock and roll and that's what I want. If you can't handle it, I'm fine with Ben. He, at least, has some manners."

"Ben's a shy, reclusive guy. It's not enough. It has to be Liam," Ian said.

Zoe's cheeks flushed pink. "But isn't it about making me look wild and impulsive? The husband shouldn't matter."

Krissy held up a hand. "Liam being his usual 'Love 'em and Leave 'em Liam' isn't newsworthy. But the infamous

Liam Jones in love? With the band's new lead singer? The public will go nuts. It's a much more powerful story."

Bitterness filled his mouth. "How long?"

Ian's eyes flared with triumph. The fucker. "For now, until the end of the tour. If it all goes as well as we anticipate, we'll reassess then."

"That's not good enough. I'm willing to do this because I want it to work. But we need some clear parameters. I don't want to have the album go platinum, the tour be a smash, and you guys keep telling us just a little longer. I gave up my public life a long time ago, but I won't let you dictate my personal life forever. So, I suggest we agree, in writing, that we file for the annulment by the end of the year." Zoe's husky voice contained a steel thread through it.

Krissy glanced down at her client, a hint of approval in her half-smile. "Fair point. How about this. We agree that at the end of the year, we will assess how everything is going. If necessary, the marriage will continue for six month incre-ments until it's viable to end it. Deal?"

Liam slammed his hands on the table and glared at her. "Not six months. Ninety day increments. And there will only be two of those and then this farce will end. Take it or leave it."

"Oh yes, you did study law in London, didn't you? Fine. That works for us, Ian?" Zoe's agent said.

Ian leaned his chin on steepled fingers. "Let's have it drafted and signed today. We've got a lot to do before you two head to Vegas on Thursday."

"Thursday? Like the day after tomorrow?" Zoe's voice sounded like she'd sucked on a helium balloon, more Minnie Mouse than soulful singer.

"I thought you had to set up the show? How the hell are you pulling that off in four days? What the fuck?"

One of the suits flashed a smile. "Oh, we arranged the

concert months ago, when we were setting up the tour. We didn't know who the lead singer would be but of course, we knew one would have been selected."

"Let's get down to specifics while the agreements are drawn up, shall we?" Ian's expression was as smug as his tone. His manager had him by the balls.

Liam knew the tour dates and had used them as part of his power play trying to force Austin's hand. It all felt different now--he'd be living a total, complete lie. Just like his whole fucking life had been a lie before he found out the truth and bailed on law school and his parents. Bile rose in his throat.

He'd do it. Because at the end of the day, all he had was Black Velvet Machine. He'd already lost it once when Tommy died and Austin bailed. He might be a loner but he needed the group. So yeah, he'd sell his fucking soul to play and perform again.

Otherwise, he had no clue what he'd do with his life.

CHAPTER 3

Zoe stared out the sumptuous private jet's window, her mind spinning the same three thoughts on replay.

One: Why had she chosen a profession where she had to conceal her true self in order to succeed?

Two: Would the current lie work and make her dreams come true?

Three: How was she going to pretend to be madly in love with Liam Jones when the guy barely acknowledged her presence?

He sat on the furthest side of the plane, headphones on, eyes closed. Like he was shutting out the whole world, especially her. Not that she was looking forward to the upcoming charade, but she was committed to it.

Shouldn't they be trying to get to know each other before the plane landed in Vegas? Ensure they appeared authentic from the start?

She indulged herself by studying him, and warmth bloomed low in her belly. Objectively, the man was one of the most handsome she'd ever seen. Spun gold curls worthy of an archangel framed a broad forehead, strong straight nose, wide high cheekbones, and a square hard jaw. His lips were chiseled and finely drawn, the only softness relieving the hard planes of his face. When he wasn't snarling or sneering, he looked almost sweet.

And the body. Ripped jeans and a faded Soundgarden t-shirt gave a deceptive image of casualness, but Liam Jones was anything but casual. She'd read somewhere that he practiced karate and yoga and his lean, finely sculpted six foot something physique looked ready to pounce, even in repose.

Yeah, she'd googled her fake husband-to-be after the fateful meeting. He'd studied law in his native England before dropping out to pursue music. He'd played with a punk band before forming Black Velvet Machine with Austin, Ben, and their legendary drummer Tommy. The band had burst onto the scene with a vengeance, racking up platinum albums, Grammys, Billboard music awards and more. They'd been hailed as the second coming of Pearl Jam, Soundgarden, and Nirvana--the renaissance of 90s alt-rock.

Now she'd not just be working with him but living with him and pretending to be his wild, infatuated wife. She sipped her vodka cranberry to soothe the sand dunes clogging her throat. Liquid courage to play this part was a necessity.

It was one thing to allow stylists to make her look like a Barbie doll in public. To perform the pop music the record company dictated they play. But she had never pretended to be in love. With her past band, the minute she'd closed her front door, the image was retired. At home, she'd never had to pretend to be someone else.

"Like what you see, darling?" Liam's emerald eyes opened. "You've been staring at me the whole flight."

Heat rose in her cheeks. "Just trying to wrap my head

around what happens when we land." She smoothed out her expression––he'd never see her distress.

He plucked his earbuds out, straightened in his seat, and dropped his elbows to his knees. "Yeah, me too."

She cleared her throat. "I mean, should we set down some ground rules or are we diving straight into PDA in the airport?"

He smirked and patted his lap. "You wanna get started on that now? Come on over."

She shook her head. "No, I'd like my last few minutes of freedom right here in my own seat, thank you very much. I meant ensure we're on the same page."

"So prim and proper. Once we step off this plane, you need to be all over me, and I plan on being all over you. Shouldn't be too much of a hardship." His eyes raked her from the top of her head, down the extremely low-cut black lace halter top she wore to her low-slung black jeans.

She had no problem showing skin––shyness wasn't in her DNA. Awareness danced along her skin––soon they would be making out all over Sin City and those huge hands of his wouldn't just be something she admired from afar.

Through sheer self-control, she managed not to shiver but her traitorous nipples betrayed her by springing to atten-tion. His gaze dropped to her breasts, and he ran his tongue along his upper lip. "Right, love?"

Two could play at that game. "You're easy on the eyes but chemistry isn't always about looks. It's more intangible."

He shrugged a shoulder. "When we played at your audi-tion, there was chemistry on stage. I'm sure it will translate. And rules––like a safe word?"

She choked on her drink. "Are you kidding with this? We'll be the infatuated couple in public. I hardly think a safe word is necessary." Was he the type of man who required one in the bedroom? Her pulse kicked in her veins.

"Look Zoe--" And once again he'd pronounced her name incorrectly, with a long "e."

She pointed at him. "This is exactly what I meant. You don't even know my name is pronounced "Zoe" not "Zoey.""

He rubbed the scruff on his jaw. "Is that supposed to sound tougher or something?"

"No, it's what my mom named me. Probably something my lover would know."

He grunted. "Fair point, Zoe."

And somehow his deep raspy voice transformed the syllable into a rough caress. Oh, she was in trouble.

The intercom buzzed and the captain informed them they'd be landing soon and to fasten their seatbelts. Zoe pressed a hand against her churning belly. Between the conversation and the impending performance she'd have to pull off in Oscar worthy fashion, her nerves were strung as tight as one of Liam's guitars.

"Okay, Krissy said they've got the driver and security waiting for us and the suite at the Virgin Hotel is ready. I guess we dump our stuff and then hit the tables? Or should we just go straight out to the Strip?"

"I'm starving, so let's eat first, hit the tables, make our mark at the hotel. Plenty of time to hit the Strip after-wards. You ready for this? Have your fans seen your new look?"

She shoved her hair back. "Some. But it's mostly going to be girls losing their mind over seeing you and wondering who the hell your piece du jour is."

"That's what the suits do the best. You don't think when they're tipping them off they'll mention you? The news today will be Zoe Gone Wild, wondering what the hell you're doing with me."

"Until tonight when a million hearts will break to learn 'Love 'em and leave 'em Liam' is off the market."

He pressed a hand to his chest. "Only a million? You wound me."

She snorted. "Oh my god. You're too much. Can't believe I fit in this plane with your ego."

"Just the facts, love. We'll have to make it good, so they buy it. Everyone knows I always swore I'd never settle down." He winked.

"We've got an unlimited budget for this charade today, right? Because I'm gonna need some top shelf whiskey to pull this off."

"Whatever you say. I don't think you'll need to act once we get going."

"Same, *babe*." He thought he was all that--and yes he was--but she had some tricks of her own. She'd have his balls so blue he'd be sobbing into his scotch.

The wheels hit the tarmac, startling her. She'd been so absorbed in their banter, for want of a better word, she hadn't even noticed the plane's descent.

Kind of like her own descent into impending madness.

The plane taxied on the landing strip. She peered out the window and sure enough, a mountain of a man waited for them beside a white stretch Bentley. Was he their driver or their security detail?

One of the benefits over the last few years was she'd been able to live without 24/7 protection. She'd loved the anonymity. Now, she looked different, she was no longer associated with the Baby Dolls, and she was out of sight, out of mind.

But if Black Velvet Machine launched again with her at the helm, she'd take the bodyguards and the paparazzi and all the negatives that accompanied mega stardom. Because she'd be the lead singer of one of the most popular bands in the world.

Well, as long as the old fans accepted her, and the new

fans came on board. Oftentimes, bands could never make it again with a new lead singer, especially after icons like Austin Michaels and Tommy Ash. But it was possible, and she was different enough to make it work. Black Velvet Machine 2.0 was the dream.

And if she had to lock lips and sit in Liam Jones's tempting lap, so be it.

The flight attendant smiled as she strolled to open the door for them. "You two are all set. Enjoy Las Vegas."

Liam appeared in front of her and extended one square palmed hand. "Shall we do this, love?" His grin was wicked.

Why did his accent have to sound so sexy saying "love?" She exhaled a fortifying breath and linked her fingers with his. A spark of electricity flashed up her arm at the contact. "Absolutely, babe."

Hand in hand, they exited the plane and strode to the waiting car. Her heart galloped in her chest and sweat prickled between her breasts. Not from the unforgiving Nevada sun, but from the connection to the golden beast leading her toward the future.

Would it be her best or worst decision?

CHAPTER 4

"Wouldn't have pegged you for the type to eat chicken and waffles."

"Yeah, you've definitely judged me correctly from the start, haven't you? Chicken and waffles is one of the greatest American dishes around. C'mon babe, don't you want a taste?" Zoe held up a forkful of chicken breast, waffle, and a strawberry, all swimming in maple syrup.

"No thanks." He shuddered.

"The waitstaff is watching and who knows who else. Don't you want to look like we're lovers?" She waved the fork around, a wicked glint in her tawny eyes.

Damn if she wasn't right. They'd attracted attention from the employees and although their table was in the back of Nellie's Southern Kitchen at the MGM Grand, a few of the other patrons kept peeking back.

"If you insist, love." He leaned in, wrapped his fingers around hers on the fork and guided the food to his mouth.

He kept his gaze locked with hers as he chewed--maybe it wasn't disgusting after all--and licked his lips. He released the fork and traced his fingers along her bare shoulder.

Goosebumps rose on her smooth skin and her nipples practically pierced through the silky fabric of her halter top.

Her pupils flared, the black almost eclipsing her golden irises.

She dropped her fork into the lake of syrup on her plate and grabbed her cocktail, her rosebud lips wrapped around the straw.

"You love the sweet stuff, don't you? The food, that sweet tea cocktail. I bet you taste sweet."

She slammed down her glass and waved to the waitress. "Like sugar. I need another drink."

"It's only 3 o'clock and our wedding isn't until 11:30 so pace yourself."

"Oh, I can handle myself, especially after I finish all this food. Another OMG Captain Jack beer?" She asked as a server materialized beside their table.

He nodded. Why the hell not? Some liquid courage couldn't hurt with the path they were embarking upon. Although the more time he spent with Zoe, the more he realized acting like he was infatuated with her wouldn't take much effort. She was hot as hell and now she'd finished her second cocktail, hints of an adorable Southern accent were slipping through her husky voice.

"So tell me why you traded in law school for rock and roll?" The flare of heat in her eyes had subsided and she merely appeared curious.

He reclined back in his seat. "Not much to tell." Or not much he wanted to share.

She sighed. "Look, if we're going to pull this off, we need to know real things about each other, okay? How about I share something first? We'll trade?"

He grunted. Somehow he had the feeling she wouldn't relent until they did.

"So, I grew up in Raleigh, North Carolina with a single

mom. No siblings. She worked two, sometimes three, jobs to help me pursue music. It's all I've ever wanted to do."

"You two close?"

She nodded. "We are. She's incredible. I wouldn't be here today if it weren't for her. What about your parents? Your family?"

"Grew up in Manchester then moved to London when I was 12. I've got a younger brother and sister. My dad's a solicitor and pushed me into law. Wasn't for me though, so I quit and here I am." Oversimplification but the facts were accurate.

"They must be proud of what you've achieved."

He snatched up his beer and downed a mouthful. "Not exactly, but not my problem."

"Okay. Was it always guitar for you?"

Music he could discuss all day. Family not so much. "Yeah. I can pull off some back-up vocals but don't really have the pipes for more than that."

"Well, you're one of the top rock guitarists of all time, so I think your focus has paid off. I'm excited to play with you."

"Thanks. Why didn't you go straight into rock?"

She wrinkled her nose. "A talent scout heard me at an open mike night when I was 16. The next thing I knew, I'd signed with the Baby Dolls. I was naïve and got stuck in the contract from hell and couldn't escape until a few years ago."

"Yeah, but why would you even sign with them? That's not a band, it's a performance troupe."

"Well, it was a lot of money and it all happened really fast." She paused and shrugged a slender shoulder. "I did it for my mom. I was able to buy her a house, she was able to go back to school and get her teaching degree, which is what she wanted to do."

Valid reasons. Just because he despised his parents didn't

mean everyone else did. "Yeah, this industry will take advantage. How old are you?"

She rolled her eyes. "Again, something you should know, right? 27. And you're 30."

So maybe he should have read the bio Ian had given him. He couldn't afford to fuck this up and the press could be relentless.

"Liam Jones. I heard you were in Las Vegas," a saccharine voice said.

Fucking hell. They'd not even been here two hours and already one of the most aggressive reporters of all time loomed over their table.

A reporter who he'd made the grave mistake of hooking up with a few years back. Once Marissa Miles had realized he wasn't planning on ever repeating their night together, she'd been on his ass. Her coverage of the band's demise had been brutal.

He glanced up. "Marissa. News travels fast."

"Aren't you going to introduce me to your friend?" The platinum blonde's eyes narrowed, and her over-filled lips curved into a fake smile.

Zoe quirked an ebony brow and sipped her cocktail.

"Zoe love, meet Marissa. She's an entertainment reporter." He caught Zoe's hand and intertwined his fingers with hers.

Marissa studied them for a moment. "Zoe Hastings, formerly of the Baby Dolls?"

Zoe gestured toward the woman with her enormous glass. "That's me."

He drew their linked hands to his mouth and pressed a kiss on Zoe's knuckles.

Marissa's nostrils flared and her gaze locked on the colorful full sleeve adorning Zoe's right arm. "Talk about opposites attract but you certainly look different these days. No more girl groups for you?"

Zoe leaned against him, nuzzled her nose along his jaw, and without looking at Marissa said, "No. But if you'll excuse us, we'd like to finish our meal."

Without waiting for a response, Zoe slid one hand up to his jaw, tilting his face down to meet hers. She pressed her parted lips against his with a throaty moan. He went rock hard instantly.

Heat flared through him, and he slanted his mouth against hers, deepening the kiss. She tasted like maple syrup and strawberries and something darker. Without breaking the kiss, he shifted her onto his lap, and slid his hands into her dark silky hair. She wound her arms around his neck and wiggled in his lap, the curves of her perfect ass digging into his erection.

Zoe fit against him like she was made for him. The world faded away, leaving only Zoe's honeyed response. When he lifted his head and looked around, it felt like he was in a trance. Marissa was gone.

Their waitress approached but stopped a few feet away from the table. "Umm, excuse me? Can I bring you two anything else?"

Zoe's unusual caramel-colored eyes opened slowly, and she ran her tongue around her cupid's bow upper lip. "Not for me, thank you."

"Just the check, please." He met Zoe's unfocused gaze—yeah, they had some chemistry, that was for sure. "Nice job."

She blinked a few times, looked around, then hopped back to her seat. "Yeah, she's a piece of work, isn't she?"

"That's one way to put it. We'll be on the evening shows for sure, and that's before we ratchet it up." A golden opportunity because Marissa would spread the word about the two of them far and wide, which was exactly what they needed.

But he dreaded seeing her again--the woman had basically stalked him for years now. Woman scorned and all that.

Zoe whipped out a tube of lipstick and slicked on bright red color. Damn, her mouth was tempting. A total contrast to the trout pout women seemed to think looked good these days. No, Zoe had a mouth like a 1920s silent film star. Kissing her wouldn't be a hardship, except now he knew how she tasted and wanted more.

Did their fake marriage include sex? He hadn't seen anything about it in the multi-page agreement they'd signed. Because now this sham seemed a bit more interesting.

"You're staring." She blotted her lips on a paper napkin and tossed it to him. "Here's a souvenir."

He burst out laughing. Ms. Pop Princess wasn't such a little prude after all. He pressed it to his chest. "I'll treasure it always, love."

She rolled her eyes and giggled. "I'm sure. I'm in the mood for tequila. Let's hit Ghost Donkey over at the Cosmopolitan and do some flights. We're supposed to get in trouble today, right?"

"Abso-fuckin-lutely. It's a fifteen minute walk, you up for it in those shoes?" Those 4-inch fuck-me heels.

"Of course. I could hike the Grand Canyon in heels. I reached my full height in eighth grade, so I'm a pro. Plus some fresh air will balance out this recycled stuff."

"It's 100 degrees in the shade." Fucking uncivilized but he preferred to walk too.

She rose and shook back her mane. "I grew up in the South where it was unbearably hot and humid. It's only a mile. Let's go, baby."

"Let's make it a memorable walk for anyone who sees us--it's work, right?" He slid his arm around her waist and tugged her tight against his side.

Her lips tightened for a moment before her face relaxed.

"Sure. We need those photos to make tonight more believable.

They strutted through the restaurant's weathered barn door and out to the garish world of Sin City. Maybe this fake relationship wouldn't be so tough, after all.

CHAPTER 5

After shooting way too much tequila, she and Liam hit the Craps table. What better game to yell, scream, and make a scene? The drinking warmed her blood and Liam's proximity heated every single cell in her body. Ever since the mind-blowing kiss at lunch, they'd been all over each other. His enormous hand skimming along her bare skin, his tempting kisses and casual caresses were escalating the tension between them. Each time she tossed the dice, he'd grip her hips and tug her against his obvious arousal.

The afternoon blurred into evening, with the cocktails flowing and the intimacy increasing. Fantasy blended with reality, and it was tough to discern what was real any longer. Around 9 p.m., she and Liam were once again at a casino bar and her phone buzzed. Krissy. She skimmed the message, grinned, and pressed a kiss to his cheek.

"Well, babe, it appears we deserve Oscars in addition to the Grammys we'll win."

He cupped her jaw and captured her lips in a deep

passionate kiss. "Gotta say, getting drunk with you is way more fun than I anticipated."

"Hey." She swatted his broad shoulder. "That's a back-handed compliment. Why wouldn't I be fun?"

He smirked. "Just thought you wouldn't be such a naughty girl."

And the way he purred "naughty girl" had her thighs clenching. "Well, you're nicer than I thought you'd be, so there. Anyway, Krissy says all the entertainment sites are blowing up, along with all kinds of amateur fan videos. The driver will be outside in fifteen minutes to take us to the Marriage License Bureau. She wants us to call her from the car."

And all of a sudden, her belly clenched. No, not from all the alcohol she'd consumed but from the reality check. Good thing she'd never been one of those little girls who'd dreamt of a big white wedding. Her dreams had been of a big spot-light. Who knew she'd have to sell her soul for the chance though.

Liam's face shuttered, he dropped his hand, and shifted back onto his stool. She shivered, the casino's air-condi-tioning chilling her skin––or was it the loss of heat from Liam?

When an uncomfortable silence replaced their banter, she inhaled a fortifying breath. *Do whatever it takes, Zoe.* "We're one step closer to re-launching Black Velvet Machine. What we both wanted."

He slammed the rest of his whiskey back and smacked the empty glass on the marble-topped bar. "Yeah. Never would've thought it would come to something like this but fuck it. You ready?" He didn't meet her gaze. Great.

"I need to hit the ladies' room first. Come with me, we still need to make a newsworthy exit, right babe?" For the first time in hours, the endearment felt forced. Bitter.

His chiseled lips twisted. "Yeah, let's do it. At least we get a little break from this bullshit in the limo."

And he was back to his asshole persona once again. He'd been having just as much fun as she had today. She caught his hand. "You've been a great actor all day, don't lose steam now."

He didn't respond, just tugged her along out of the loud bar toward the restrooms and toward their sham wedding.

Once they tumbled into the limo, he sat at the far end, rifling through the crystal liquor decanters. All the warmth and laughter of the day had vanished into some black hole and now Liam was back behind that ice-cold demeanor.

Moody bastard.

She called Krissy and put her on speaker. "Hello, you two lovebirds. Fantastic job so far. You even had me fooled."

Liam glowered at the phone, as if Krissy could see his murderous expression. "Yeah, well, this plan better fuckin' work."

Krissy's tone chilled. "It's working much better than the crap you pulled. You're lucky Austin didn't sue you for giving that interview, when you knew perfectly well he wasn't returning. In fact, you're lucky you're getting a chance at all."

Liam's nostrils flared and his fingers tightened around the decanter.

God, she hated confrontation. "Now now, kids. Just a few more hours today and tomorrow we get to hide out in our suite, right? Don't worry, Krissy, we've got this."

"I knew I could count on you, Zoe. First, Harry Winston is staying open late just for you. Your rings are ready. You'll pick those up and head to get the license, I finished up your online application. The press knows, so make it look real, like you've been doing all day. Then, onto A Little White Wedding Chapel. You'll have to wait for the drive-through like everyone else. Any questions?"

Liam poured three fingers of whiskey and raised a brow. She nodded. The only way the rest of this night was happening was by getting good old-fashioned drunk. And they were well on their way. Although she'd been alternating glasses of water, so she didn't pass out or puke before the big event.

"It's crystal clear. And tomorrow and Saturday we lay low in the suite and meet up with the guys to rehearse for the show, yeah? All of that sorted too?" Liam handed her a full glass before crossing one foot over his knee.

"It is. The guys will arrive tomorrow afternoon and we've got studio space reserved for you. The limo will pick you two lovebirds up at 2 o'clock. Make sure to flash those rings on the way, but no need to talk to any of the reporters."

Once they rang off, the adrenaline from the day dissolved and she melted into the buttery leather upholstery, like a deflated balloon. When they'd been in the moment, they'd had fun. Their chemistry was off the charts and kissing and touching Liam Jones was no hardship, as countless women were aware.

Now, she couldn't wait until this charade was over. At least when they returned to their suite, they had separate bedrooms and she'd avoid him as much as possible until rehearsal. For the last two years, she'd had the freedom to be herself and not slap on her public persona. She'd forgotten how exhausting it was. And Liam wasn't making it any easier with his attitude. Like somehow this whole charade had been her idea.

They'd only been faking it for one day. How in the world was she going to continue this charade through the end of the year?

And no way would she think about that dilemma now. She exhaled a shaky breath, leaned forward, and flipped on the radio. Of course, an old Black Velvet Machine song filled the air. She glanced at Liam, whose eyes were now closed, his leonine head resting back on the seat, lines of exhaustion bracketing his mouth.

So they'd sit in silence.

The limo purred to a stop outside the back entrance of Harry Winston Jewelers and the chauffer escorted them inside.

An elegant brunette brought out the rings and placed them on the glass top counter. "Here's your selection. Double check to make sure they fit properly."

Without glancing at her, Liam picked up his ring. "I'm sure it's fine."

So she'd be sliding her own engagement ring on her finger. How romantic. She sighed and picked up the ginormous diamond ring that should be in a museum. Holy hell, what had Krissy been thinking? Totally not her style.

She tried it on, and it fit perfectly, although it felt more like an anchor weighing her down than a symbol of commitment.

Probably because it wasn't a true commitment.

"You ready?" Liam glanced at her ring and up at her.

She nodded and thanked the woman. Without another word, they returned to the limo and headed to pick up the marriage license. Her earlier pleasant buzz was officially gone.

"You going to be able to keep this up? Because that was pretty pathetic. Let's hope she doesn't spill to the press." Because she was giving this whole situation everything she had and he was already acting like a spoiled brat.

He raised a golden eyebrow. "Like I said, taking a break from the performance."

She huffed out a breath. "I know you're angry about all of it, but it's not my fault. Keep your attention on the prize—the band's comeback."

"Oh really? If we didn't have to rehab your image, we wouldn't be on the way to a fucking wedding chapel."

Annoyance flared inside her. "It's just as much your problem since you basically committed fraud. So get off your high horse, do your part, and stop acting holier than thou. It's not like this is the first time you've lived a lie."

His nostrils flared and he sat up, his spine ramrod straight. "You don't know what you're talking about. I gambled about Austin. It could've worked. But your entire career was a lie——your image was fake. I've never acted like someone I'm not. I'm a prick and everyone knows it. So get over yourself. I'll turn on the fucking romance when there are people around. Otherwise, this is me."

"Well, lucky you, getting to do whatever you want. Some of us don't have that luxury." No way would she admit she'd started liking him. That she was really attracted to him. That his kisses and their banter had felt real.

Obviously, she was deluded on top of everything else. Was this really going to be worth it? She had to marry this guy and live with him? Talk about the ultimate sacrifice.

He shrugged and reached for the whiskey. "You don't know anything about my life. And it doesn't matter. Let's just get this done and get back to the hotel. I'm wiped out."

He poured them both another drink, handed her a glass, and sat back and sipped his own.

They stopped at the marriage license bureau, where some photographers lurked by the entrance. Liam wrapped her in close to his side and they hurried into the building as the flashing bulbs sparked like fireworks beside them.

Fortunately, the line was short, and she kept her face pressed into his hard, hot body, with his arms keeping her close. When it came time to sign their names on the license, Zoe's fingers shook.

Liam's face was pale, beads of sweat adorned his forehead, and if her imagination wasn't playing tricks on her, his long fingers trembled too. Not so cool and collected now, was he? Once they completed the paperwork, they sprinted to the limo, and ignored the shouted questions from the paparazzi.

Mission accomplished. Now for the real performance: exchanging wedding vows.

The limo pulled up to A Little White Wedding Chapel's' Tunnel of Love. Now she could relate with Alice falling down the rabbit hole. Talk about surreal. Although the minister would perform the ceremony through the window of their vehicle, they still had to go inside to sign paperwork.

When they returned to the limousine, time slowed, like she was swimming through a dream or Wonderland. The desert heat contrasted with the frigid air-conditioning in the vehicle, leaving the fabric of her top clinging to her skin. Her limbs grew heavy, her throat felt full, and the interior of the Bentley felt like a tomb.

Too late to run now. She took a few fortifying breaths. This sham marriage, although over-the-top, was the right thing to do for her, for Liam, and for the band. And it was temporary, like everything in life. Only temporary.

The officiant, an elderly gentleman with a dramatic comb-over, appeared, along with a short round little woman with hair a shade of red not found in nature. "Hello there, Liam and Zoe. Can you please both sit over here next to the window so we can perform the sacred vows and you two can drive away united as one?"

Zoe scooted in close to Liam, the heat from his skin warming her, the hint of whiskey on his breath strangely tempting her to kiss him again. Yeah, not the best idea.

She placed one hand on his muscular thigh, smiling to herself when his muscles tensed beneath her fingers. Not so indifferent to her touch after all.

He placed one hand over hers and squeezed.

The officiant smiled at them. "Lula here will be your official witness. So, without further ado, we are gathered here today…"

His words filtered in and out of her consciousness, again like a dream. But then he said her name and she focused.

"Do you, Zoe, take Liam to be your lawfully wedded husband, for better or for worse, in sickness and in health, until death do you part?"

Her heart galloped in her chest. *Death? It's all a performance. Use your training, girl.*

She turned and met Liam's shadowed emerald eyes. "I do."

He sucked in a sharp inhale and his fingers tightened over hers.

The officiant repeated the vows to Liam, who gazed into her eyes and said, "I do."

"Wonderful. You may kiss the bride." The old guy clapped his hands.

Liam slanted his mouth against hers. She melted into him and her lips parted, deepening the kiss. Sparks danced along her skin and heat bloomed in her belly. No question their chemistry was real.

The officiant cleared his throat. Loudly. "Congratulations. We'll be right back with your certificate. Go ahead and exchange your wedding rings. Hold tight."

He hurried back into the small building, their witness trotting along by his side.

Liam reached for the bag containing their rings. He turned toward her with the small velvet box. "Give me your left hand."

She swallowed and complied, despite her unsteady hands. He slid the ring onto her finger, and it snapped in place with the finality of a key turning in a lock. The coolness of the platinum band against her over-heated skin and the weight of the J.Lo worthy stone somehow rendered the entire situation even more real.

Time to break the tension. She waved her hand under the overhead track lights of the limo, the sparks blinding in the dim light of the interior. "I'm not sure if the diamond's big enough, can't believe you skimped."

Liam's lips twitched. "We Brits aren't like you Americans with the giant diamonds. I mean, who would've thought ten carats wouldn't satisfy you? Besides, your hands are tiny."

"No excuses. And your turn." She pulled his ring out of the other jewelry box. Also platinum, it had a meteorite black stripe through the middle. "Yours is very rock and roll. It will compliment your skull ring."

When he reached for it, she shook her head. "No, my turn."

He extended his powerful artistic hand, and she slid the ring in place. Just like her own, it fit like it had been custom made. Without releasing his fingers, she lifted her gaze to his.

His eyes were hooded, his jaw tight. For a moment, they simply stared at each other. Tension thickened the air, and everything intensified. The intimacy of the moment was overwhelming, and words failed her.

He cleared his throat, then pulled away. "Another drink?"

Suddenly exhausted, she shook her head. "I feel pickled straight through from this day. A bottle of water would be great, though. Do we have any?"

"Good call. Water it is. I'm ready to be back in the hotel and go to bed."

His words hung in the air.

"Not together. We've got our own rooms. And this marriage is on paper and in public but is not real behind closed doors." He headed to the other end of the limo and fetched them two bottles of water.

"Of course. The honeymoon suite will be our safe zone."

The officiant chose that moment to appear and offered her the certificate. "Okay, congratulations, Mr. and Mrs. Jones. May you have a long and happy life together. Good night."

"Thanks and good night." She stared down at the certificate showing both of their names and the words "holy matrimony."

"It's done. Let's get back." And with that romantic comment, Liam reclined against the smooth leather seat and closed his eyes.

Talk about anticlimactic. She stared out the tinted glass window as the chauffeur navigated out of the Tunnel of Love back to their hotel. Yeah, she'd been used to draconian contracts stealing her freedom, but this was next level.

And the rest of their lives.

Or the next six months, whichever came first.

CHAPTER 6

*L*iam knew he was being a hypocritical asshole. Here he'd been condescending to Zoe about her choices, and he'd just fucking gotten married in some spot called the Tunnel of Love. And he couldn't squash the thoughts crowding his brain and the uneasiness roiling through his gut.

Was the band worth all the sacrifice? What if the fans didn't care? If it was all too late?

Well, at least Nevada law had broad annulment rules. If he ended up lumped together with fucking Britney Spears under short-lived Vegas marriages, he'd personally ring Ian's neck.

The limo purred to a stop in front of the hotel. Show time. The chauffer opened the door and Zoe stepped out first, and waited for him, their marriage certificate clutched in one hand. The overhead lights bounced off her diamond ring, almost blinding him. Holy hell, the thing must've cost a cool million.

"You ready for our grand entrance, wife?"

Her whiskey eyes widened. "We're making a grand entrance? I thought you just wanted to get back to the room."

"Oh I do. But we've come this far, so we may as well go all in. Tradition dictates I carry you over the threshold, right?" Fuck it, if his career was exploding into flames, he'd make it good.

Her pink lips formed an "O" and she gasped.

Before she could utter a sound, he swept up her curvy little body into his arms. Her full breasts smashed against him, and he held her tight. She pressed one small hand against his chest and tilted her head up at him. "You're crazy."

He leaned down and murmured against her lips. "It's showtime, love. Let's show everyone here just how crazy we are for each other. Hold on tight and make sure to flash that ring so everyone can see it."

Her fingers grabbed a fistful of his shirt, and she wiggled her perfect ass against him. He went hard instantly. Again. Between her intoxicating jasmine scent and her satiny skin, the clanging bells and too-bright lights faded away.

He strode toward the elevators. Maybe this idea had been smarter in theory than in practice because all he was doing was getting turned on. Not good when their relationship was for public consumption only. Even though he'd had one of the most fun afternoons of his life with her "acting" like a couple. Zoe Hastings was a fascinating woman, and her creative mind and resilience drew him to her.

In private, he needed to keep his distance because obviously, their explosive chemistry could only spell trouble. Sex would complicate the next year way too much. But for the walk to their suite, he'd torture himself with the feel of her. Yeah, he was a masochistic idiot.

The murmurs morphed into catcalls and by the time they reached the elevators, recognition had kicked in. "Liam.

Liam. Liam Jones, ohmygod, she's got a ring on. Is he married?"

"Who's the woman? Who is your bride, Liam? Tell us. Tell us." The crowds surged toward them and by the time he'd stabbed the elevator button, they were surrounded.

Zoe pulled his head down for a kiss, then turned to the throngs around them as the elevator doors opened. "You can call me Mrs. Jones, Zoe Hastings Jones."

Casino security appeared, working to disperse the crowd. Cheers and congratulations filled the air as they backed into the elevator, ready to escape. As the doors slid shut, Liam's gaze snagged on a platinum blonde shooting daggers at them with her eyes. Marissa. Well, now the shark reporter had her scoop, and the story would be everywhere.

Yeah, the band's managers would be thrilled. Maybe he'd killed two birds with one stone. Gotten that woman off his ass finally and shared the marriage immediately.

"You can let me down now, it's just us." Zoe pressed her hands against his chest.

He shook his head. "No can do, darling. There are cameras in the elevators and I'm carrying you over the threshold." And maybe he loved the feeling of her in his arms.

She struggled against him. "Put me down." Her eyes were golden halos around huge pupils, and her cheeks were flushed.

"Impatient, aren't you? We're almost there." Yeah, he should put her down, but his hands refused to comply. Being this close to her scrambled his brain and all the reasons to maintain a safe distance from her fell away.

"Fine, have it your way." She grabbed his face in her hands and nipped at his lower lip.

He hesitated, then backed her up against the elevator wall. One hand slid up to fist in her hair and he cupped her ass with the other. She shifted and wrapped her legs around him, her sharp heels digging into his back. The heat from her center burned against him.

The elevator bell dinged, but damned if he wanted to stop.

Damn if he could stop. Not with her eager response.

She shifted her mouth away from his. "We're here. Take me to our room." Her voice was whiskey on silk.

He backed up a few steps, shifted her into his arms, and strode down the hallway to their suite. He fumbled for the key, yanked it out of his back pocket, and waved it in front of the door.

He carried her across the threshold into their suite, headed straight for his bedroom, dropped her on the bed, and dove after her. He propped himself up on his forearms and gazed into her heavy-lidded eyes. Her breath came in shallow pants.

"I need to see you. I have to taste you." If he didn't, he'd lose his mind.

"Yes," she whispered.

He shifted to one side and unbuttoned her pants, sliding them down her smooth pale thighs, revealing a tiny thong. A tiny soaking wet thong. He groaned and tore it off. "Take off your shirt."

She obeyed, pulling it off over her head and tossing it to the side. He ran one hand lightly from her delicate collarbone, down her dangerous curves, then cupped her. "You're fucking perfect, love."

"Liam."

He tugged her to the edge of the bed, slid down onto his knees between her thighs and gazed up at her. "I'm going to make you come apart. Tell me you want it."

Her hips rocked up. "Please."

"Lay back, watch me and enjoy, beautiful." He pressed her

thighs apart and stroked one finger along her center. She was pink and perfect beyond his wildest dreams.

Her back arched, and she gasped when he slid one finger inside her. Then two.

"You're so wet. So ready for me." He lowered his head and brushed light, open-mouthed kisses along her clit and she moaned.

He lowered his head and licked her in one long stroke. She bowed up, his name escaping her lips. He circled his tongue along her sensitive bud, tasting her, savoring her. He worked her hot tight center, finding the spot to drive her wild.

"You taste fucking incredible." He murmured against her, never lifting his head. "Come for me, darling."

"I'm so close. Please don't stop. Please." Her legs were vibrating, and her hips rocked against his mouth.

He reached one hand up and pinched her rosy nipple and she exploded. "Oh yes, oh my god Liam, yes."

He didn't stop as she came apart and when she stilled, he lifted his head and smiled. "You're the most delicious thing I've ever tasted in my life."

And it was the truth. Holy shit, it was like Zoe was made for him. He stiffened as the realization rolled through him. Where had *that* come from? He sat back on his heels and scrubbed his hands through his hair.

She propped herself up on her elbows and patted the bed beside her. "Come here."

Unable to resist her, he climbed up onto the bed.

"How am I naked and you're still fully dressed?" She pressed one small hand against his rock hard erection. "Let me return the favor."

She licked her lips and he almost exploded. *Dangerous.*

Time to create some distance between them. Slow things down. Even though all he really wanted was to bury himself deep inside her and fuck her until the sun came up. But she was his new bandmate. His fucking temporary wife. Not one of his usual hook-ups. He couldn't forget it.

He pressed a light kiss to her tempting lips. "Tonight is about taking care of you. I'll be right back."

Her dark brows drew together. "Are you turning me down?"

"Just taking a rain check, darling. I'll be right back." He must be out of his fucking mind. But his gut told him it would be a mistake to get any more intimate with her than they already were. Something about her made him feel out of control. And it scared the shit out of him.

She huffed out a breath, punched the pillow behind her, and curled on her side. "Fine."

His lips twitched and he strode to the bathroom to shuck his clothes and calm down. Zoe wasn't just sexy and talented; she was charming and adorable too.

Yeah, Zoe was dangerous.

He returned to the bed, and she was sound asleep. He climbed in beside her and prepared for a long sleepless night.

Yeah, maybe this was penance or maybe he was just an idiot.

CHAPTER 7

Zoe blinked the sleep from her eyes and gazed around the hotel room, completely disoriented. Awareness dawned at the hot, hard male imprinted against her back, his legs tucked beneath her bent ones. She looked down at the sinewy arm wrapped possessively around her waist. Liam was draped around her like a vine.

They'd spent the night together in his bed. Spooning. Spooning naked. What had they done? Or more like what hadn't they done?

Her heart thundered in her chest, and she eased Liam's arm off her, slowly scooting away. He grunted and his long guitarist fingers tightened on her belly. *Crap.* Right now, she couldn't face him, not after the memories poured into her brain.

His golden head buried between her legs.

His talented tongue.

His wicked fingers. And his oh so naughty words.

Yeah, he'd given her the most amazing orgasm of her life and then acted like a gentleman, tucking her into his arms and falling asleep.

She wasn't sure if she should be insulted that he'd declined her offer of reciprocation or touched that he'd been considerate enough to suggest they wait to go further. Who would have believed "Love 'em and Leave 'em Liam" was a giver? And a cuddler?

But she needed to pee, find her clothes, and escape to her own room to pull herself together. In that order.

Holding her breath, she tried again.

"Hmm…" He grumbled under his breath but didn't move.

She managed to untangle herself from his embrace and collected her clothes from where they were strewn around the room. Her shredded thong dangled from the lampshade. Although she'd loved it when it was happening––her cheeks flamed. She tip-toed into the suite, crossed to her room, and shut the door.

A long, hot shower helped rinse off the whiskey hangover and Liam's scent from her skin. How was she going to face him this morning and during rehearsal? Time to dig deep for all her performance skills, the acting ones, not the singing ones.

In a few hours, they were meeting the rest of the band at a small studio. But first––sustenance. Liam was likely as ravenous as she was and they both needed to soak up yesterday's drinking binge. She ordered a vat of coffee and enough food to satisfy a family of six from room service.

She took her time drying her hair and applying a full face of makeup. Today, she needed the confidence of a smoky eye and perfect skin to project her new image as Black Velvet Machine's lead singer. And, well, sometimes her appearance acted as armor, and she had a feeling she'd need it when she saw Liam.

A loud knock sounded at the suite door, and she hurried out of the bathroom.

Liam beat her to it, dressed in low slung jeans and a snug

black t-shirt that highlighted his rangy frame. He directed the server to set up the table by the vast floor-to-ceiling windows which brought in the cerulean desert sky.

He glanced back at her, one brow raised. "Thanks for ordering breakfast or should I say lunch? I called down and you'd already done it. I'm starved."

She joined him at the table. "I figured today would be a long one and I can't function without caffeine and food."

"Aha, good to know. We're meeting the guys over at the studio in an hour. That enough time for you?"

She nodded. "I just need to throw on some clothes after we eat and I'm good to go."

His gorgeous green eyes darkened and dropped to the fluffy hotel bathrobe she wore. With nothing under it. "Brilliant."

And why did she have to reference her nakedness under the robe? She lowered her gaze to the mountain of scrambled eggs, bacon, toast, and potatoes. They navigated the meal with small talk and technical logistics about today's rehearsal and tomorrow evening's show.

Easier to ignore all the other topics like the fact they were married, the fact they'd fooled around last night, and the fact they'd spooned like a couple in love. Yeah, better to overlook all of that.

Oh my god, in the space of a week she'd been hired as lead singer for one of the biggest rock bands in the world, gotten married in Vegas, and was going to perform with the band at The Theater for an exclusive audience. All the food she'd wolfed down shifted and she pressed her hands against her churning belly.

"You okay, love? You look a little pale--feeling all that whiskey?"

She cleared her throat. "Everything that's happened this week is all hitting me at once."

He set down his fork and his jaw softened. "Yeah, it's a lot. But it's all happening, and we'll find our rhythm in rehearsal, you'll be amazing, and tomorrow's show will blow everyone away." His tone was gentler than she'd ever heard.

Her shoulders relaxed. "Thank you. I want that more than anything. I don't want to let you guys down or let the fans down."

Liam's phone buzzed and he picked it up off the table. "It's Ian." He rose and stalked over to the windows. "Yeah?"

Zoe couldn't follow the conversation because Liam's responses were monosyllables. Yes, no, and grunts. And perhaps she was admiring the way his black t-shirt emphasized how his broad shoulders tapered to a narrow waist and spectacular butt. No question the man was hot, hot, hot.

He pivoted to face her and slid the phone into his back pocket. His expression was inscrutable. Liam could probably rake in millions at the poker tables downstairs.

"Anything important?"

He raked his fingers through his golden hair and blew out a breath. "I guess. He and the team are pleased at how yesterday went. We are apparently the top story on all outlets. Lots of speculation about how we met, a lot about you…"

"About me, what?"

"Don't shoot the messenger okay?" He held up his hands. "But they're comparing you to Britney Spears several years back when she got married in Vegas and shaved her head and all that."

She jumped up from the table. "Britney Spears? Are you kidding me? Wasn't this plan just supposed to make me seem like a wild rocker chick? Not an out of control pop princess? What did they say about you?"

"More speculation about us getting married––was it just

a drunken escapade we'll get annulled by next week. That there's no way we would actually stay together."

"Great. That's just fantastic. My mom is probably losing her mind."

"You didn't tell her?"

"No. The only people who know are the band and our management teams. The fewer the better. The paparazzi will hound her and it's better she not know. I don't want to put her in the position to have to lie." Now her breakfast threatened to exit via her throat.

"You said you two are close?"

"Very. Like I mentioned, she sacrificed so much for me to have a singing career."

"Well, then you should call her. Just tell her it was…tell her it was love at first sight."

She snorted. "This all happened so fast, I didn't have time to think all this through. Not sure she'll buy it. She knows me too well. Is that what you're going to tell your family?"

A shutter came over his face and he shrugged. "We're not close."

Hmm…time to explore that later. "I'm going to have to figure out a way to talk to her without lying." She sank into a chair and dropped her head in her hands. Yeah, this plan was way more complicated than she'd considered.

"Well, if you're calling her, make it quick because we've got to get over to the studio. And we need to sneak out the private exit to avoid the press. Can you be ready in 15?"

"I'll text her not to worry, that I'll call and explain it all tomorrow. And yeah, I'll be ready." She rose and returned to her room, her heart racing, her palms sweating. Her mom understood what she'd endured in the Baby Dolls and would be heartbroken for her if she learned she'd married to promote her career.

Why was this career such a juxtaposition between bitter and sweet?

~

"And here's the happy couple now," Ben clapped, and the rest of the guys joined in, whooping and crowing like die-hard football fans at the Super Bowl.

In addition to the band, a sound engineer, a producer, and Ian crowded into the space.

Liam slammed the door behind them and muttered under his breath. They'd ridden over to the rented studio in relative silence. He'd seemed as lost in his thoughts as she was, and the lack of conversation had been comfortable rather than awkward.

Please, universe, don't let the next two days be a nightmare.

She held up one hand. "Guys, can we save all the enthusiasm for when we're in public? Let's make the rehearsal about kicking ass tomorrow night and leave the rest."

"We've got to play a part in all of this and I, for one, am going to have fun with 'Love 'em and Leave 'em Liam's' demise." André winked.

Liam flipped the drummer off and picked up his guitar. "Yeah, yeah. Have your fun, you fuckers. And if our fans find out this isn't real, Black Velvet Machine is done for good."

Ben shrugged a shoulder. "We got it--you two just couldn't wait. Soul mates and all that shit. Don't worry, we'll pull it off. And thanks for taking one for the team, man."

Liam grunted.

Yeah, surly guy was back. Zoe gritted her teeth and dumped her fire-engine red satchel on a table against the wall. Time to focus on why she was here--the music--and tune these guys out. Because they were acting like Liam was a martyr and what, this was just par for the course for her? *This is my dream gig. This is my dream gig.*

She didn't know any of them yet and it wasn't the time to assert herself or express her own feelings about any of it. She needed to show them she could be the lead vocalist for the band, and as a woman, she had twice as much to prove. Not just in the entire music industry, but in the group. She hadn't driven through that wedding tunnel to lose out on this opportunity.

"Okay guys, how do you usually run things?"

Ben walked over and handed her the set list. "I think it makes sense to practice the songs in order. Take a look and let us know if there are any on here you don't know."

She skimmed the list, which consisted of many of the band's top hits ranging from anthems to a few ballads. Her song, *Shine*, which she knew would vibe perfectly with the band's signature sound, was conspicuously absent. Krissy had confirmed she'd sent it over after they'd signed the contracts. It was part of the deal.

"I've got a handle on them, some more than others. But where's my song, *Shine*?" She forced herself to slow her breathing down and prevent the irritation flickering up her spine to flare into anger.

"What song?" Liam's brow furrowed.

"The song that is part of our agreement. I wrote it. We're singing it tomorrow night and if it goes over well, it's going on the album."

Ian finally raised his head from where he'd been fiddling with equipment. "Yeah, you guys and girl should close with it. The list should have been updated."

"You're kidding, mate, right?" Liam scowled at Ian.

And her irritation blazed into a raging inferno.

She stomped toward Liam. "Not kidding. You've been

playing the BVM songs for years so you should have the bandwidth for one new song."

"It's not exactly fucking ideal. Like we don't have enough to pull off without a song we didn't write?"

"I. Wrote. The. Song. Aren't I the lead singer of the band, *babe*?"

Before Liam could respond, Ben stepped between them. "Hey, everyone hold on. Liam, shut the fuck up. Ian, you should have given us a heads up before today."

Ben pointed a finger at her. "Zoe, calm down. You have to agree the timing's a little rough for tomorrow night. Can it wait until the tour?"

Zoe's hands curled into fists, her fingernails digging grooves into her palms. "Look, guys, I'm part of the band now. If we come out for the first show in over three years and I sing only your material, it'll seem like I'm just a fill-in. Not the new lead singer."

"But we're playing one of the new songs we wrote, already the fans won't know the difference," André said.

"This is the perfect opportunity to cement that I'm the new singer, that my material is part of the band. I mean, like we aren't going to be under a microscope with the marriage?" She scanned the room. "You can handle a three minute song. If this is going to work out, we need to work together."

Ian marched to the middle of the room. "It's not a question. It's what's happening and it's part of the deal. I'll give you the music at the first break and you can review it. So quit your bitching and get your equipment set because we're starting in ten minutes, period."

Tension permeated the air and for a moment everyone remained rooted to their spots.

Liam shrugged and his pissed-off expression smoothed

out. "Zoe's right. We'll learn the song later today and high-light it at the show. For now, let's do the set list in order."

Zoe's shoulders softened and relief flooded through her. Liam had stepped up––not exactly a given––and the rest of the guys followed his direction. It felt good to have him support her, but would every single event with this band be a battle?

She'd won this round but how long was she expected to fight before she'd be accepted?

CHAPTER 8

*L*iam's gaze swept the small stage. Only one minute until the curtains pulled back for Black Velvet Machine's return show. The 4,600 person venue was packed, and the crowd noise was deafening. The standing room, seats, and luxury suites buzzed. Beads of sweat prickled on his brow and he wiped them away.

Not as overwhelming as when they'd played stadium venues, but tonight's intimate gig was the perfect way to re-introduce the band to the world. Their first performance without the incomparable Austin up front. Without the incomparable Tommy pounding the drums.

But André was legit with the sticks and Zoe brought a new energy to the band, one he'd not anticipated. And judging by how she had killed it during rehearsal, despite the circus surrounding them, tonight would kick off a new era. A different era.

A fresh start.

Since they'd arrived at the studio yesterday until tonight, he and Zoe hadn't had a moment alone. Initially, they'd planned on being "seen" again last night but after twelve hours of rehearsal, everyone had returned straight to the hotel and crashed.

Ian insisted he and Zoe should play up their relationship during the show. A kiss here, a stroke of her hand along his shoulder, long, lingering looks between them. More acting. More performance that had nothing to do with their sound.

His gut clenched--if he hadn't needed this band like he needed oxygen--he'd bail. Factor in his very fucking real and very fucking unexpected attraction to Zoe and he was a mess. Would liking her make the acting part get easier as time went on?

In the end, it would all be worth it, right? The new album would hit platinum fast, they'd have a successful tour, and then Zoe and he could return to their "normal" lives after a quiet annulment.

"Rock and Rollers, for the first time in more than three years, and for the first time with lead singer Zoe Hastings, I introduce to you Black Velvet Machine," the emcee shouted, effectively shutting off his meandering thoughts.

Show time.

The lights flashed, André beat on the drums, and the crowd roared. The band sounded tight, the acoustics were incredible, showcasing the riffs, the rawness of the music, and the mesmerizing range of Zoe's voice. Like they'd been playing together for years. Her performance hypnotized the crowd who sang along, danced, and some fans even sobbed with joy.

Adrenaline coursed through his veins and the power, the intensity, the sheer fucking joy of performing the music he loved so much for an enthusiastic audience again filled him. Damn, he'd missed the connection of a live performance.

Song after song, his awareness of the fire in Zoe's eyes and the passion behind her performance surged. Sweat glistened on her ivory skin and her ebony mane was wild around her face. And yeah, the memory of how she tasted was close to the surface.

They reached the end of the set, and it was time for Zoe's song. He strummed the opening chords, and she sauntered over toward him on her five inch heels, owning the stage with her confidence and skill. She ran one hand down his bare arm, and he went stone hard. She turned to the pulsating crowd, who had not only accepted her but fucking loved her voice and energy.

She was a live wire, owning the stage.

"So, I've got a special song and I'd like it to dedicate it to this guy right here. Does anyone know why I'd do that?" Her voice was flirty, throaty. Sexy as hell.

Shouts came from the packed venue--he could see the whites of some of the fans' eyes, the place was so crowded. "You love him!" "He's your lover!" "You two are married!" "Because he's hot AF!"

She threw back her head and laughed. "You're all right. Because this sexy beast right here is my husband. Maybe we're playing with fire by working together and by..." She looked around, her ebony brows raised, working the crowd to perfection.

More screams and howls, "Tell us, tell us!"

She pursed her cupid's bow lips and blew them a kiss. "No, no, I don't kiss and tell. This song is called *Shine* and it's about letting go of all the crap that weighs you down, that dims your light, and choosing to shine your brightest to the world, no matter what. If Liam Jones doesn't personify shining bright, there's no hope for the rest of us, right babe?"

She smacked his ass and sashayed away, in a blur of black leather and dangerous curves. The crowd roared their approval, and he focused his gaze on his guitar strings and launched into the brilliant opening riff of Zoe's song.

She worked the stage, belting out the lyrics all while

strutting and swaying to the beat. She moved like a dancer—— all grace and power. Had she danced? Whether she'd been trained or not, she was the sexiest most powerful thing he'd ever seen. She lifted the fans up and soothed them down, finishing the song next to him, one small hand on his shoulder.

The crowd thundered and stomped on the floor, screaming for more. The curtains fell and Ben and André joined them to take a final bow. When the drapes parted again, the applause and screams continued. They bowed and waved and sauntered off stage, Zoe's hand clasped in his. Their connection felt real. Despite how much of the rest of it was fake, fake, really fucking fake.

"You were incredible." He whispered the words against the silky skin beneath her ear. "Fucking magic." He'd under-estimated every single thing about this woman.

Her lips curved up and she squeezed his hand. "We were incredible. I loved every second of it."

Black Velvet Machine 2.0 was back, and judging by the audience's reaction, Zoe was the right choice.

When the band reached the alcove where the press awaited them, he pulled her in close to his side. Champagne was on ice and a fine bottle of Macallan had his name on it in the band's back room but first, they had to answer some questions. Make it good for the public and set up the new album and Fall tour.

Ian had set up a podium——at least they had a small phys-ical barrier from the upcoming onslaught. He gazed around the people holding out microphones and shouting questions. Then, he caught sight of Marissa, her calculating narrowed eyes scanning between him and Zoe. *Shit.*

Time to take charge before the reporters went rogue. Before Marissa spewed her usual venom. He held up a hand.

"Hey everyone, we've got time for a few questions. Quiet

it down for a sec and we'll get started. How about you?" He pointed to a wiry bald guy he recognized from one of the major music sites.

They alternated answering questions about the upcoming tour, how they chose Zoe, and other softballs--nice and easy. Even though he hated dealing with this aspect of the industry, the reporters were keeping the questions to the band for the most part.

So far, so good. His shoulders relaxed.

Ian stepped in, "We've got time for one more question."

"What's the deal with this marriage? It sure seems like a publicity stunt to get attention for the band. 'Love 'em and Leave 'em Liam', how long have you known Zoe?"

And there she was, Marissa, trying to stir up trouble. No way was that scheming bitch messing this up for them. Zoe stiffened and he tugged her in closer and pressed a kiss against her lips. He knew how to handle the piranha in pink.

He grinned down at Zoe. "Black Velvet Machine returning with a new album and tour doesn't need a publicity stunt. You can retire my old nickname because I've got no reason to leave. Zoe's the first woman who ever made me want to stay, so I figured I'd make it official."

The press began buzzing and shouting out more questions.

"You want us to believe you fell for some pop princess?" Scorn laced her tone. Yeah, Marissa was livid. She could go screw herself.

"Who wouldn't fall for this woman--she's got a hell of a voice, she's tough as nails, sweet as sugar, and she's all mine." He hugged Zoe in closer.

Zoe sucked in a breath and held up one hand. "That's *former* pop princess to you, sweetie. Time marches on so feel free to come along for the ride or not. You can call us the King and Queen of Rock and Roll now."

Ben, André, and Ian all shouted and hooted, "Hell, yeah. Queen Zoe!"

Time to wrap this up. "Thanks everyone. We'll see you on tour. It's time for us to celebrate. Black Velvet Machine's back."

More questions and calls rose from the media pack, but Liam was ready for a drink or ten. Time to make an exit the media wouldn't forget. He turned to Zoe, and scooped her curvy, warm body into his embrace.

She wound her arms around his neck and pulled his head down to hers. "Thanks for standing up for me," she murmured against his mouth, her breath sweet and hot.

"Anytime, darling. Let's give them a grand farewell and get some whiskey. That was a hell of a show."

She wiggled her hips and pressed one hand against his heart. "Okay, Your Highness."

He puffed out his chest and strode toward their after-party room feeling better than he'd felt in…ever?

What was this surprisingly complicated woman doing to him?

CHAPTER 9

"Mom, I know what I'm doing. I know the marriage was fast. Yes, it was impulsive but that doesn't make it a mistake." Zoe paced around the perimeter of the enormous, sunny bedroom.

"Honey, I love you and I'm worried. The only time you ever brought a boyfriend home to meet me was when you were in sixth grade and invited that little hooligan Jeff Hawkins over. Fifteen years later you marry a man two days after meeting him? What's really going on? All these nasty stories claim you're out of control. That your marriage is a publicity stunt."

Zoe nibbled on her lower lip and paused to stare at the deep blue Pacific Ocean outside the wide window. She'd never lied to her mom before. Her mom was her best friend. But she'd signed an NDA and she was actually protecting her mom by keeping her in the dark.

Yeah, sure, keep telling yourself that.

"I love you, Mom. The reporters are exaggerating and blowing everything out of proportion. They should be focusing on how fantastic our show was and how Black

Velvet Machine is back, not the marriage. There are some…
ahem…circumstances. Please believe me that you've got
nothing to worry about. I promise I'll explain everything
when I come visit you."

Her Mom pounced. "I? Don't you mean we? Aren't you
bringing Liam home to meet me?"

Crap. "I'm still getting used to being part of a couple. Of
course, once we've finished recording the album, I, I mean
we, will have time to visit. We're working around the clock
to wrap as soon as possible. Once it's done, I'll have time
before we go on tour."

Silence. After a few beats, her mom responded. "Okay, I'm
not going to push you. But you promise me one thing."

"Anything." *Except admit my marriage is a publicity stunt.*

"I'm always here to listen, day and night. I really hope this
whole quickie marriage isn't another manipulation by the
band or your PR people to sell records. You've already spent
years playing a role. You deserve to be recognized for your
talent. Full stop."

Yeah, wouldn't it be nice to simply be a lead singer
without an elaborate public image. But the fake marriage
plan was working, just like the PR people said it would. This
band was her chance to fulfill her dreams of singing rock and
roll--her way. When she was on stage or downstairs in
Liam's state-of-the-art recording studio, she was completely,
totally the authentic Zoe Hastings.

"Thanks, Mom. I completely agree I deserve it. Black
Velvet Machine is my chance. I know what I'm doing." The
sacrifice was worth it. Would be worth it. The marriage was
temporary. She would keep her eye on the long-term prize.

"You're not pregnant, are you?"

Zoe's mouth dropped open. "Mom, no, I'm not pregnant.
And even if I was, I wouldn't feel compelled to get married.
Sheesh."

"Okay, okay. Just checking. Well, good luck recording. I'm so proud of you, honey. I love you. Call me soon."

"I will. I love you too."

She tossed the phone onto the King sized bed, leaned against the window frame, and soaked in the breathtaking view. Liam's Spanish style mansion sat high on a bluff, with views of the rugged Southern California coastline. Towering palm trees, jagged cliffs, and pounding surf. Time to pull it together and return to the studio.

"I didn't think you were involved with anyone?" A gruff British accent said from behind her.

She whirled around and Liam stood in the open doorway, looking deliciously disheveled. He wore his usual dark jeans and concert t-shirt, today's was The Doors. His golden hair needed a trim, and a few days of scruff darkened his chiseled jawline.

"Ooh, is my husband feeling possessive?" She raised an eyebrow.

He strode into the room, his eyes narrowed. "I just heard you tell someone you love them. We're married, so that's a problem."

"Aren't you in a mood today?" And why did the idea of him feeling possessive kick up tingles in her belly?

He stopped a few feet away from her and scrubbed his hands through his hair. "Sorry. So who was it?"

No need to tease him further. They had a full afternoon and evening of recording ahead of them. Even though a teeny part of her enjoyed his apparent discomfort.

"Don't worry, hubby. It was my mom. And it was a tough conversation because she cannot figure out why I'd get married in Vegas so quickly, but I couldn't tell her the truth."

His thick brows drew together. "Yeah, that is tough. Did you figure out a way to avoid lying to her?"

"Yeah, I skirted around it and was really vague. But it

looks like we're going to visit my mom after we finish the album."

He paled. "Visit your mom?"

She threw back her head and laughed. "I never thought I'd see the infamous Liam Jones scared. My mom is awesome. We'll deal with the it when the time comes. No need to worry now. But you know, spouses usually meet the in-laws."

He hissed out a breath. "I haven't seen my parents in years, so that's not happening. Fuck, this is getting complicated."

She approached him, her footsteps muffled on the gorgeous indigo area rug, and gazed up at him. "It was never simple." And he was right because she was starting to care about him.

"Let's go back down to the studio. The guys are ready to get back to it." He turned to the door, and she fell into step beside him.

The band. Time to focus on the end goal. They crossed through the middle courtyard of Liam's home, and through a wide buttercream-colored hallway with high ceilings and white-oak floors. Sounds arose from the open doorway leading downstairs to the vast, modern recording studio where the rest of the band, sound engineer, and Ian awaited them. Time to tuck away her discussion with her mom and shift her focus to the music.

"There you two lovebirds are," Ian winked. "Everything's set up for *Shine*, but I've made a few tweaks, so it sounds more consistent with the rest of the record."

Zoe's temper flared. Again? "I thought we'd settled that the song would be recorded how I wrote it. How I intended it?"

Ian shook his head. "Just a few minor things. Take a look."

She marched over to him and snatched up the paper, struggling to keep her anger under control. Maybe it was something minor she could live with, but hadn't she sacrificed enough? Her song's inclusion was part of the whole damn contract.

Liam had followed her and read over her shoulder. "Those aren't little tweaks. You changed the bridge."

She flung the sheets onto the counter. "And the chorus. You've changed the whole feel of the song. No."

Ian held up both hands. "The essence of the song will feel the same, you'll see. You're new to the alt-rock——"

"Don't patronize me, Ian. I am not new to the genre." Heat suffused her cheeks and her hands curled into fists. No way would she allow the management to manipulate her music. Never again. She was already sacrificing her personal life for the band. They would not sacrifice her song.

Liam stepped in. "Absolutely not, mate. You heard her. We'll record the song the way Zoe wrote it. Not only is that stipulated in the agreement, but we discussed it. We performed it and the fans loved it."

Ian opened his mouth to respond.

"Agree with Liam and Zoe. The song's awesome as written." Ben folded his arms across his chest.

"Me too. We're unanimous and it's our decision. We want to do *Shine* the way Zoe intended." André had crossed the room and stood behind her and Liam.

Warmth filled her——Liam had stood up for her. The guys had backed her up too——maybe they truly were becoming a group.

Ian's nostrils flared and his voice was controlled. "Fine. But I think you're making a mistake. No offense, Zoe, it's a good song, I just wanted to make it great."

Zoe managed not to tell Ian to go fuck himself——very mature of her. "Duly noted."

Liam brushed her shoulder and smiled down at her, his

green eyes gleaming. "It's a great song so let's play the hell out of it. Guys?"

Ben and André high-fived and returned to their spots. They would record the instrumentals first and then she'd lay down the vocals. She strolled over to the refreshments table and poured herself a cup of tea and added a generous dollop of honey. Her throat was parched from all the difficult conversations, but she'd be ready to sing her song. Her way.

Liam believed in her and hadn't hesitated to stand up to Ian on her behalf. Not that she couldn't fight her own battles--she'd been doing it her whole life--but her heart was full. She wasn't accustomed to people having her back, especially not someone like Liam. Underneath his gruff exterior, Liam was a good guy.

Yeah, his comment about their relationship being complicated was the simple truth. Because her feelings for the cocky Brit were becoming more complex each day.

CHAPTER 10

"Water or champagne?" *Or me?*

"Let's finish the bubbles first. Because we've got the house to ourselves, finally." Liam lounged against the black granite topped island in the center of his massive chef's kitchen. He looked delicious in faded black jeans and a snug Iggy Pop t-shirt.

"Excellent choice." She grabbed the bottle from the ice bucket and topped off their glasses.

Her fingers brushed against his and every nerve ending in her body sprang to life. She retreated a step and sipped the crisp liquid. Over the last week, the tension between them had escalated second by second. Working with him in the studio had been stimulating and illuminating. His focus, his talent, his determination to ensure every single song was the best the band could produce revealed the depth of his dedication.

They'd worked sixteen hours a day with minimal breaks to wolf down a quick meal. The rest of the band and the production crew were staying at Liam's Spanish-style mansion and believed their marriage was fake. When she and

Liam finally collapsed into bed at night, they stayed in their separate bedrooms. But tonight, everyone needed some space and the rest of the guys had gone out.

Now it was only her and Liam.

Alone.

Despite the sheer physical and mental exhaustion, her fascination with Liam had grown exponentially. Beneath his brusque exterior, he was clever, passionate, intense, yet fair. He'd stated he didn't talk to his family--were they the reason he kept most people at arm's length? When he was making music, his guard was down, and she'd never been so attracted to a person in her life.

More than the physical, she actually *liked* Liam.

Plus, the way he'd insisted the band would record her song without the changes Ian tried to push, touched her heart. He'd not only seen her vision--he saw her. He believed in her. He'd fought for her.

"Thank you again for standing up for me with *Shine.* It means a lot."

He angled toward her; his emerald eyes gleaming in the light. "The song is perfect how you wrote it. It's a bit of a departure from our usual sound but we want that. We need your influence to show the band is evolving."

Had he realized he'd referred to the band as 'ours?'

Her heart knocked against her ribs and heat blossomed low in her belly. "Liam, kiss me."

His eyes hooded and he pounced. With one swift move, he picked her up and placed her on the smooth countertop and stepped between her legs. She wrapped her legs around his lean waist and tingles blazed along her spine at the hard, hot feel of him.

He fisted one hand in her hair and tugged her head back, then lowered his lips to the hollow of her throat. She moaned. He nibbled up the sensitive skin on her neck and, with a growl, slanted his mouth across hers. Their tongues danced, and stroked, and she savored the tart flavor from the champagne on his warm breath.

"You taste like heaven," he murmured against her mouth. He slid one hand up and cupped her breast, brushing his thumb across her taut nipple.

Her back bowed and she braced her hands on the cold granite counter, giving him access. With a growl, he lowered his head and raked his teeth across her nipple through the whisper thin silk of her tank top. Goosebumps danced along her skin and fire coursed through her veins. "Liam, oh my god."

He tugged the fabric aside and his mouth captured her breast. She dug her hands into his soft hair, holding him in place. "Oh yes, so good."

He cupped her through her jeans, and she rocked into his hand. Needing more.

He stroked his fingers along the seam of her pants and her hips bucked. "I can feel how hot you are. You are so sexy."

Shivers wracked her body and she moaned. She needed more. She scrambled to unbutton her jeans, to eliminate the barriers between them. "Please help me get these clothes off."

He growled and stepped back, made short work of her pants and thong, and tossed them aside. He spread her legs apart with one hand on each thigh. His pupils flared, "Zoe, you're fucking perfect."

He stroked along her center, and explored her with long, blunt fingers. He pressed the heel of his hand against her clit, then slid one finger inside her. Then two. His talented fingers stroked and played her like he already knew what drove her crazy.

Waves of pleasure pumped through her system. He captured her mouth again and their kiss grew wild as she rode his hand, all sensation centered on his hot mouth and his calloused hands.

"Come for me," he murmured in his sexy as hell accent without lifting his lips from hers. "Come now, love."

And with his murmured command, she came apart, lights bursting behind her eyes, sparks flaming along her slick skin. Her mind blanked and she went limp in his arms.

"Wrap your legs around me." He grasped her hips and lifted her from the counter.

Her limbs obeyed and her eyes flew open. His skin was flushed, and his eyes were feral. He captured her mouth again and strode out of the room, hopefully to his bedroom. Because the steel ridge of his erection digging into her was too much temptation.

"I want you inside me. Please tell me you have a condom," she whispered against his lips.

He lifted his head, his jaw tight. "Darling, I do and you're about to get what you want."

He dropped her onto his bed, and she melted into the cloud soft comforter and mattress. With one hand, he ripped his t-shirt off, tugged at the button of his jeans with the other, and stripped off his pants and black boxer briefs. He strode to the nightstand, yanked open the drawer, and tossed three condoms on the bed.

Her breath came in staccato beats, her pulse hammering against her throat. Her mouth grew dry at the sight of him naked. His body was a work of art, chiseled pecs, long lean abs, and carved V-muscles descending to his huge beautiful cock. She licked her lips.

He joined her on the bed and settled on top of her, bracing his forearms on either side of her. She looped her arms around his neck and arched against him, savoring the feel of his naked body against hers. He lowered his head and captured her mouth in a deep, searing kiss.

He brushed his lips down her neck, leaving a trail of fire along her breasts, scraping his teeth along her sensitive peaks. Her hips slammed into his and she moaned his name. But he didn't stop his teasing torture.

He lifted his head and flashed a wicked grin. "Want me to keep going?"

"No, I need you inside me now, please." She raked her fingernails lightly down his spine.

"When you say please…" He shifted, lean muscles rippling against velvet skin, and grabbed a condom.

He knelt between her legs and together they sheathed him. He caught her hands, intertwined their fingers, and plunged into her in one masterful stroke.

"Give me a second." Her breath caught at the exquisite fullness. His thick hard length felt like he'd been made for her.

He held still and reached one hand to smooth her damp hair away from her face. "You have any idea how incredible you feel, Zoe?"

"You feel so good." She gazed up into his gorgeous green eyes, overwhelmed with the feeling of connection.

"Ready?" he rasped.

"Yes, please." Her eyes floated shut and her head dropped back onto the pillows.

He began to move in long, powerful strokes. She wrapped her legs around him and lost herself in pure pleasure. The room filled with sounds of their heavy breathing, their bodies moving, and their skin went slick and hot.

He slid one strong hand beneath her, tilting her up and creating a delicious friction that rocketed her to a climax again.

"Liam, oh my god," she lost control and flew over the edge again.

"Zoe," Liam followed her over with a roar.

After a few moments, he shifted and rolled them to the side, pulling her close against him. She pressed kisses against his sweaty, solid chest and allowed the afterglow to sweep over her.

She tilted her head back. "So, yeah maybe we have a little chemistry."

A surprised laugh escaped him, and he stroked his magic fingers down her spine and cupped her ass. "Yeah, maybe a tiny bit."

They grinned at each other. "Hold on a minute and let me take care of this. I'll be right back."

She admired his chiseled physique as he strode to the bathroom. Wow, wow, wow. Their interlude was hands down the most incredible sex she'd ever experienced. With her husband. *Gulp*.

When he returned, he pulled her back against his front, and wrapped one sinewy arm possessively around her waist. Somehow, despite their height difference, they fit perfectly together. She relaxed her head against his strong shoulder and melted into his warm embrace.

Now they'd actually consummated their sham marriage. And it hadn't felt like casual sex--it had been raw and emotional. Their pretend arrangement had become very, very real. Nevada's annulment laws were lenient, but each day they spent together was one more day as a married couple. One more day falling under Liam's spell.

She was a big girl. She could handle it, right?

CHAPTER 11

"And that's a wrap," Ian called from the sound booth.

André banged out a dramatic ba-da-bing on the cymbals, Ben pumped one fist in the air, and Zoe shouted, "Yes."

Satisfaction filled Liam. The album was great. Fucking great. All of them could feel it. Zoe had stepped into her role as Black Velvet Machine's lead singer with ease and style.

Time to celebrate—he strode across the room, caught Zoe's gorgeous face in his hands, and slanted his mouth across hers. He needed to feel her delicious body against his. He'd become addicted to her jasmine scent, her soft skin, and their passionate lovemaking.

His guitar created an unnecessary barrier between them, so he whipped the strap off his shoulder and set it aside. She looped her arms around his neck and dove into his kiss.

Over the last few weeks, his perspective on Zoe—hell, on life—had altered dramatically. Their days were spent downstairs in his recording studio where the album had come together smoothly and swiftly. Their evenings were spent upstairs in his bedroom. Once everyone turned in, Zoe would tip-toe to his room and the secretiveness made their nights even hotter. The made-for-the-public marriage had morphed into something more.

Flames radiated down his spine and the room faded away. All that mattered was Zoe. He had been dead fucking wrong about her before—she was real. Not manufactured. The most genuine person he'd ever met.

Unlike his dishonest parents who'd never revealed the truth about his real father and probably never would have if he hadn't overhead them, Zoe didn't keep secrets.

Like she'd said before, her Baby Dolls image was purely for public consumption, and she'd kept her personal life private. She'd done what she had to do to take care of her mom and he respected her sacrifices.

"Whoa, no cameras in here, kids," Ian said.

"Get a room!" Ben hooted.

Zoe recovered first and backed out of his arms "I can kiss my hubby if I want. Hell, I'll give you all a kiss."

She sashayed over to André and pressed a kiss on his cheek, then followed suit with Ben.

Liam's eyes narrowed when Ben pulled Zoe in for a hug. What were his bassist's hands doing so close to Zoe's perfect ass? He wanted her by his side. He wanted her in his arms. Damn it, he wanted Zoe, period.

His heart kicked against his ribs and sweat prickled between his shoulder blades. Holy shit, was this what falling in love felt like? And where the hell was all this coming from?

She tossed her hair over her shoulder. "Sorry Ian, no kiss for you."

Ian barked out a laugh. "Zoe, your voice and your performance are all I need. You're fantastic and this new album is going to relaunch the band into the stratosphere."

Her cheeks pinkened. "Thanks, Ian. I feel honored to be a part of it all. So, we're finished recording?"

"Yeah, like I said, that's a wrap. It's all in the mixing and editing now. You guys can take a break while we get started on that."

Liam shook his head, needing to regain a sliver of self-control. "You know I'm always involved in the post-production and I'm sure Zoe wants a part, right?"

Her golden eyes warmed and she beamed at him. "It was never an option with my former group, and I'd love to participate."

"Yeah, that's fine. But all of you take a few days off. Maybe go out and celebrate somewhere tonight. Let the press see you all together, and you crazy kids just keep kissing for the cameras. Let's keep building the hype."

Zoe's grin faltered, but she recovered quickly and glanced around the room. "Of course, it's been a while since Vegas. I'm down for getting dressed up and hitting the town together."

"Sure. Let's take the limo and head down to Nobu in Malibu, sound good?" Ben asked.

"Just make sure the limo's stocked with Johnnie Walker Blue and I'm down," André said.

"Liam?" Zoe tilted her head, her eyes questioning.

Liam gritted his teeth. "Yeah, okay." He hated the reminder their relationship was for the press. And he was in major trouble.

Ian clapped his hands together. "I'll make the reservation for 9 o'clock and have the driver pick you up at 7:30. Again, thanks for all the hard work. We're back in business."

Everyone started packing up their gear and clearing out. It was already 6 o'clock.

"Is it cool if we crash here one more night, Liam? Easier with the limo and then we can move back to our places tomorrow," Ben said.

He shrugged. "Yeah, no problem."

Finally…he and Zoe wouldn't have to sneak around anymore. Because nobody suspected how close he and Zoe had become. It wasn't like they'd discussed the fact they'd become truly involved, not even with each other.

Maybe it was time for them to talk. Maybe it was time for him to confess how their connection was more than sex. More than the music. She was one of a handful of people he trusted––she was the truest person he'd ever met. She had to feel the same, right? He couldn't be the only one catching feelings, could he?

"Meet you guys down in the kitchen at 7. I'll mix a pitcher of my world famous margaritas for the road." Zoe waved a hand and sauntered out the door without a backward glance.

Yeah, maybe Zoe wasn't as invested as he'd assumed? Or was she just a better actress? Either way, they had hours with the band before a discussion was an option. He scowled.

"Dude, don't look so pissed off. Pretending to be Zoe's husband isn't exactly a hardship. Wish the team had asked me to do it." Ben winked at him.

"Fuck off. Not a hardship. Just hate the b.s. with the media, that's all." He set his Gibson back onto its rack and headed out of the studio.

The guys made kissing sounds and André called after him, "Liam loves Zoe."

He flipped them off and stalked out the door.

Yeah, if they only knew.

LIAM'S SELF-CONTROL was about to snap. The evening had been one endless, agonizing ride. From the moment Zoe had strolled out of her bedroom wearing a black leather dress with a slit up to the top of one creamy thigh and a neckline that plunged to her navel, he'd been rock hard. All that soft gorgeous skin on display begged him to touch her.

Now she was plastered against him in a corner booth, with one delicate hand resting on his thigh. Unable to resist, he dropped a kiss on her bare shoulder and inhaled her jasmine scent. She shivered and her fingers tightened on his leg. Yeah, their chemistry was over-the-top. He'd never survive this interminable dinner--maybe he could convince her to meet him in the restroom and take her against the wall.

She threw back her head and laughed, her throaty voice another layer of temptation. Every muscle in his body tensed. Yeah, her voice when she was singing or laughing or moaning his name drove him wild. This woman.

Yeah, his heart was involved. Even though at the moment, his dick was ruling his system and all he wanted was to get the hell out of this fishbowl and back to his house. Just the two of them.

He leaned in and brushed his lips against the side of her slender neck. "Can we get out of here? I want you to myself."

Her pulse hammered in her throat, revealing she was affected as he was. She nodded and murmured, "Absolutely. We've done our duty and the guys want to keep partying. Let's take the limo back and they can call a car service."

"Done." Oh, he'd make sure she enjoyed the limo ride back to Santa Barbara.

He straightened in the seat, ready to bolt out of the restaurant, pronto. "Guys, Zoe and I are headed back to my house. You cool with us taking the limo?"

Ben nodded. "Yeah, I'll call a driver I work with to take André and me down to Melrose. You sure you two lovebirds don't want to come?"

Zoe laughed again. "We don't want to cramp your style."

"Never. We're stoked you're one of us now, Zoe. We've got all the time in the world to party when we go on tour."

Liam rose and tugged Zoe to her feet and toward the exit. "Later," he called over his shoulder.

"Someone's eager," Zoe purred and snuggled in closer to his side.

He pressed a kiss to the top of her head. "Oh yeah, just you wait until I get you in the limo."

They reached the door and she paused. "Kiss me."

He turned her into his arms, slid his hands into her lush mane, and lowered his mouth to hers. She hummed deep in her throat and wound her arms around his neck. He sank into her soft curves, savoring the tartness from the margaritas melded with her sweet flavor.

Flashing lights exploded, followed by people screaming their names, and shouting questions. "Liam and Zoe!"

"Smile for the camera!"

"Zoe-am!"

"How's married life, Li-oe?"

"You two just posing for the camera to convince the world you're really together? What's the real story?" A sharp female voice barked.

Zoe froze and they retreated into the lobby. "Text the driver to meet us in the back. Hurry."

The manager ran up, apologizing profusely. "Please, go to the private exit. We'll get rid of the paparazzi. I'm so sorry."

Liam didn't have time to waste on him and led Zoe to the other exit at a half-jog. A fine sheen of sweat covered her brow and her lips flattened into a tight line. Goddamn press.

Fortunately, Nobu was accustomed to celebrity clientele, and they managed to reach the limousine without further incident.

Zoe practically dove inside, and he slid in beside her. She

dropped her head into her hands, her dark hair forming a curtain obscuring her face from him.

He stroked one hand down her back. "Sorry, love. I wasn't thinking. We should've gone out the back."

"Well, Ian and the team will be thrilled, I'm sure. They probably tipped them off we were there." She sat up and her head dropped back against the seat.

He blew out a long exhale. "Yeah, I'm sure they did. It's just me and you now." Yeah, not exactly how he'd envisioned their ride home.

She tilted her head toward him, her caramel-colored eyes shadowed. "I'm not sure it's ever going to be just us."

He picked up her hand, drew it to his lips, and pressed a kiss to the center of her palm. "There's always a new story. We'll be forgotten soon."

She frowned. "I know we signed up for this, but I didn't realize it would be so hard. It was one thing to play a part for the Baby Dolls onstage because it wasn't personal. This is our real life, you know? I'm having a really hard time keeping it all separate."

A burst of protectiveness tugged at his heart. "Yeah, it is real, but it will be okay. We'll be more careful. Once the album's out and we're on tour, the music will take center stage and they'll let us be."

"I don't know, Liam. Me and you together is juicy news. I'm exhausted." She withdrew her hand and interlaced her fingers together on her lap.

She closed her eyes, effectively shutting him out. All the thrill and excitement of the day disappeared. He wanted to comfort her and didn't know how.

In another first, he didn't know what to do at all.

CHAPTER 12

"Ⓘ'm sorry, but I need to be alone tonight." Zoe pressed one hand to her roiling belly. Margaritas, sushi, and paparazzi were not an ideal combination.

Something flared briefly in Liam's green eyes. "If that's what you want."

"It's not what I want," Wasn't that the truth? "It's what I need. It's all getting to me, and I just want to take a bath and sleep. Okay?"

And here she was patting herself on the back for being so honest. What she needed was Liam to hold her in his powerful arms and convince her it would all work out. For him to tell her he was falling in love with her too.

"You know where my room is if you change your mind." His accent was clipped, all British aristocracy suddenly. He turned on his heel and strode away.

Her heart plummeted. He hadn't even tried to change her mind. And wasn't she a bundle of contradictions? He'd done what she asked. She should be relieved.

But she hadn't been dishonest about feeling awful. Over the last few weeks, everything had become real between them. At least on her side. She was falling madly, deeply, irrevocably in love with Liam Jones.

Spending time with Liam was easy. Natural. His grouchiness had almost disappeared, at least with her. He still snapped and barked at Ian and the sound engineer if the sound wasn't perfect. But now she recognized part of his gruff demeanor was tied to his quest to honor the music.

In the studio, they meshed better than she could have imagined. His talented fingers strumming the melody she wrote? Catnip.

Singing the words to a haunting ballad he'd penned and expressing the emotions he kept buried beneath his tough guy exterior? Kryptonite.

Laughing when they messed up, cheering when they hit the perfect notes.

And their nights, their forbidden perfect nights after the rest of the band had gone to bed. Hot, dirty sex and tender lovemaking. Steamy, slippery showers together. All of it combined packed an emotional punch.

Tonight's media ambush was a sobering reminder of what was at stake. Not just her career, but her heart. And call her a coward, but right now, she had to protect herself.

What was that famous Maya Angelou quote? Something about when someone shows you who they are, believe them the first time. On day one, he had declared he liked his "Love 'em and Leave 'em Liam" nickname.

Because while Liam obviously cared for her, and shared their once in a lifetime chemistry, he'd made it clear love and marriage weren't in the cards for him.

Well, real marriage, anyway.

She had to create some distance before her heart shattered. She'd believed she could pull off the fake marriage for her dream job. Hell, she'd given Oscar-worthy performances with the Baby Dolls for years. But playing a pop princess had been superficial--a masquerade that ended the moment she was in the privacy of her home.

Falling for her fake husband was a deep dive she wasn't sure her heart could recover from. It had only been weeks--no way could she continue for a year or longer.

She picked up the phone and dialed Krissy's number. Her BFF and agent was a night owl, so a 1 a.m. phone call wasn't out of line.

"Zoe, are you okay? I saw the latest with you two getting mobbed at Nobu."

"I am definitely not okay. And seriously? Already?"

"Of course, I've got alerts set up on you two so anytime you're mentioned, I'm pinged."

Zoe cleared her throat. "Well, that must be a nightmare. Anyways, I need your help."

"Anything. What's up? Congrats on finishing the album. Ian said the tracks are fantastic."

She sank into the cushy softness of her bed, the one she hadn't slept in for weeks, and closed her eyes. "The album is going to be amazing. It's the rest of it. I can't pretend to be married to Liam anymore."

"What happened? I'll kick his ass if he's being a jerk to you."

She choked out a laugh. "It's not that. Liam's incredible."

"Really? So you two are getting along now?"

Time to confide Krissy about just how well she and Liam had been getting along. They had been living in a beautiful bubble at his home, safe from the outside world. But now she needed help.

"Okay, I'm speaking to you first as Krissy, my friend. Second as my agent. Promise me you will not reveal a word of what I'm about to say. To anyone."

"Of course, I won't. I can't believe you think I would."

Zoe released an unsteady breath. "I'm falling in love with

him, and I cannot stay here any longer or I'm going to end up broken hearted. You need to help me figure out a way out of this. I just can't do it."

The line was silent for a moment. "Oh Zoe. So I take it this means you've been sleeping together?"

She threw an arm across her face. "Yes. But more than just mind-blowing, life-altering, ballad-worthy sex. He's so intelligent and funny too. He stood up for me to Ian and insisted my song be recorded exactly as I wrote it. He insisted I'm part of the editing process. He brings me breakfast in bed. He listens to me. He sees the real me. And he's protective and sweet. We've really connected. I like him. I'm falling for him. And I can't handle it."

Krissy coughed. "Sweet? I'll take your word for it that he's different behind his rocker persona. Have you told him how you're feeling?"

"No. I haven't wanted to ruin it. But the record's done and now it will be just the two of us in his house and I'm scared. You have to help me." Zoe's heart squeezed in her chest.

"Okay, okay. Although I think you two should talk. What if he feels the same way? Don't you want to know?"

"Look, he made it clear he never wants to get married and have a family. I mean, he's said that in more than one interview. He doesn't even talk to his parents. It's just too dangerous for me."

Krissy sighed. "Well, there's a way but it involves you acting unstable, and you'll have to play it up in public, so I don't know if you'll want to do it."

Her throat tightened. Nope, she had to protect herself. "Tell me."

"We can file for an annulment now. You'll need to make some kind of scene, either a public fight with Liam or you acting erratically solo. Something to make it clear the marriage is over."

Numbness flooded her body. "I doubt Liam would agree to staging a fight. And I don't want to blindside him."

"Yeah, you're probably right. I don't think he has your acting chops. So, you tell him the plan––maybe just say I suggested it to add even more interest in the band and the tour because fans will dig the drama. And if any questions remain that you're too popstar, this will cement you belong in rock and roll."

Zoe pressed one hand against her chest. "In my mind, I know you're right. But in my heart it feels terrible. But it's safer this way. When?"

By following her agent's advice, she'd redirect the bulk of the press's attention to her and away from Liam, which he'd appreciate.

"Well, it's the weekend. But I can prep the legal filing and we'll leak it to the press. I'll just need you to check in to Chateau Marmont and get wasted in Bar Marmont for the world to see. Be loud and obnoxious. Maybe kiss another guy?"

"No, I'm not going to kiss another guy. Drunk I can do. Or at least pretend to be drunk. Oh this stinks." A sharp staccato beat raced in her temples and bile rose in her throat.

"It's going to be okay. Liam can handle it. Tell him the deal, pack up your stuff, and head over there in the afternoon, okay? I'll take care of the rest."

"Okay. Thanks Krissy."

Her friend made it sound so simple. And maybe it would be if she didn't care. She didn't want to hurt Liam, but she had to protect herself. It was for the best. For both of them. For the band.

Although, one part of her whispered he would be upset because even if he wasn't capable of falling in love, he cared for her. She'd make him understand it was for the best. After all, she'd been a good actress in the past. She could be one again.

He'd never wanted the fake marriage and he'd probably be relieved.

Now, she'd take that long bath and try to sleep.

Tomorrow, she'd break the news to him before she left.

CHAPTER 13

*W*hat the actual fuck? Liam threw his coffee mug across the kitchen and savored the dramatic crash when it shattered into a thousand pieces.

"What was that?" Ian asked.

He ground his molars together and glared at the phone. "Nothing. So Zoe's leaving my house today, and everything's already set up for her to make a scene at the Chateau?"

Sure would have been nice if she'd bothered to tell him. So this was why she'd wanted to sleep solo last night. How long had she known? Was this the strategy all along?

"Yeah, Krissy called me first thing to tell me the new plan and it's brilliant. I know you weren't keen on this whole fake relationship and now you don't have to pretend anymore." Ian chuckled. "Her acting erratically will work great for the press. I don't know how I didn't think of it first."

Smug bastard. Liam stalked to the window and glared at the postcard view and pristine blue sky. Fuck this sunny state. He needed to return to England or move to Seattle where the gray, dark weather suited his mood.

"Liam?"

"Yeah, I'm here. Anything else?"

"That's it. Maybe lay low for a few days. The press will show up outside your gates and try to catch your reaction. But once the initial news dies down, the focus will be on Zoe, and she can handle it. She's a pro from her time with her former group."

"Yeah, no problem. Gotta go." He tossed the phone onto the counter and paced around his kitchen.

Why had she gone behind his back? Zoe had confided in him how much she hated living a lie. He'd trusted her. He'd been about to spill his guts that he was falling for her last night, and she set this up without telling him?

He'd been right--he couldn't trust anyone. She'd been the first person he let his guard down around and she'd been planning on bailing once the record was finished? Had the timing of the annulment been part of her plan all along? Without discussing it with him. It felt like a dagger to his heart.

"Liam? What happened to the wall?"

Speak of the devil. He pivoted to face her and schooled his expression. "Don't worry about it. Heard you're leaving today so it's not your concern."

Her face paled and her golden eyes widened. "You know? I was just coming to talk to you about it. I--"

"Save it. Ian told me so don't bother. I'm going down to the studio." His heart tugged in his chest, but he squashed the emotion.

No way he could deal with her explanations. Listen to her or look into her eyes.

"Liam, will you please listen?" Her voice came out on a whisper.

He averted his gaze and strode past her. He called over his shoulder. "Goodbye, Zoe."

He marched downstairs and slammed the door closed

behind him. Locked it for good measure. Not that Zoe would chase after him. He was a fucking fool--he'd allowed himself to care for her and she'd lied to him, just like everyone else in his life.

He grabbed his guitar. Nothing helped him escape his dark feelings more than music. Nothing good could come of him brooding about Zoe and the clusterfuck that was his life right now. He'd been right from the beginning--the only thing that mattered was the music. He should be relieved about the annulment.

So why did he feel like shit?

THREE HOURS LATER, Liam's fingers hurt, his eyes burned, and his stomach protested his failure to eat today. He'd played every savage riff he knew from the Rolling Stones to Led Zeppelin to Guns n' Roses. Lyrical solos, angry jams, and everything in between. Well, except for any of Black Velvet Machine's songs.

For a few blessed hours, he'd channeled his mood through his guitar and now was pleasantly numb. Zoe had to have cleared out by now, so he'd head upstairs and make a sandwich. He unplugged, placed his guitar back on its rack, and took the stairs two at a time.

His house was quiet for the first time in weeks. The guys must've come and picked up their stuff or they were sleeping off last night. Either way, he was alone. Just like he'd wanted.

After a quick peek at his security cameras, he was satisfied the press weren't camped outside his gate. Yet.

He strode into the kitchen, whipped open the fridge and pulled out bread, ham, cheese, and spicy mustard. He tossed the basic ingredients onto the granite island and turned to grab a knife. And there, propped up on the counter, was a square ivory envelope with his name on it in sprawling script. Her engagement ring sat beside it.

"Damn it." He threw back his head and roared.

Unable to resist, he snatched up the note and tore it open. One folded sheet of rich parchment paper. He lifted it to his nose and inhaled the faint hint of jasmine. A visceral wave of longing filled him. Part of him wanted to toss it in the rubbish but he had to read her words.

Liam,

I'm so sorry you heard the news before I could speak with you and explain why I chose to leave. I've loved spending time with you, and I treasure our connection. I know together we can make Black Velvet Machine the best it can be.

But the paparazzi is so relentless and the pressure on us is excruciating.

I know you never wanted to play a part and the scene at Nobu made it clear to me that the press will never stop hounding us. At the end of the day, it's my reputation that we need to change. So let me take the brunt of it.

Krissy suggested the annulment would make me appear as even more of a "bad girl" and allow you to step back and do what you do best--play music. So, you're off the hook. No more pretending to be mine. I hope once your anger subsides you see how this is best for all of us.

Yours,

Zoe

Yours. He re-read the note. Read it again. And read between the lines. Damn her for running away. Because she was his. And he was hers. Sweet, authentic Zoe hadn't been playing him. What an idiot he was for even considering it.

His ego had reacted first, along with the eighteen-year-old boy whose life had changed in a flash when he'd learned the man who'd raised him wasn't his father. That his parents had lied to him his entire life and if he hadn't overheard their discussion, he never would have known the truth.

So yeah, he had major trust issues. But who wouldn't be upset after what he and Zoe had shared?

Zoe was the most authentic woman--most authentic person--he'd ever met. Her feelings hadn't been fake when they were alone together and neither had his. Their connection was real. It went way beyond the mind-blowing sex and into how she made him feel cared for. Safe to be himself with her. And he was in love with her.

Everything had happened so fast, and they hadn't yet built up the kind of communication they needed because their relationship started as a PR stunt. But if he could convince her to try, he knew she'd work on their marriage with the same effort she put into what was important to her.

And he wasn't going to allow her to run away.

No way would he agree to an annulment. And he knew just how to convince her to make it real.

Sandwich forgotten, he ran downstairs to the studio and grabbed a pen and piece of paper and began to write.

CHAPTER 14

Zoe swiped some salt from the rim of her Cadillac margarita and lifted her finger to her lips. The great thing about Chateau Marmont was it was filled with celebrities. So at the moment, nobody was paying attention to her. It was only 4:15 p.m., so Bar Marmont wasn't crowded yet.

Earlier, she'd checked into a suite, showered and changed into a miniscule excuse for a dress. Thigh-high scarlet leather boots that matched her lipstick, messy black eyeliner, a floppy black hat à la Stevie Nicks, and it was showtime.

If she was about to make a major scene, she may as well do it in style. But there wasn't enough tequila to make her feel okay about it. She'd already decided to pretend to be drunk because if she really did get wasted? Well, everyone knows liquor is truth serum and she'd start proclaiming her love for Liam Jones instead of advertising their epic break-up.

Krissy was tipping off the press for a 4:30 scene, so she had time for one stiff cocktail for courage. Easy to pretend she'd already been drinking. She'd slurred for the cute young wannabe actor tending bar. Setting the stage and all that.

Her stomach clenched again. What a nightmare this morning had been. Ian was a major pain in the ass. He just couldn't give her time to tell Liam herself. The flash of pain in his bottle green eyes kept replaying in her mind. Had she made a terrible mistake in not talking to him first?

Well, no going back now. The stage was set. She still hadn't come up with a plan. Celebrities went wild at the Chateau, so she needed to stand out beyond the regular nip slip or epic make-out session. Climb onto the bar and dance? Yell out to everyone to join her in a toast? Her throat grew parched.

Maybe she did need more liquid courage than she'd anticipated.

She picked up her cocktail and downed half of it in one sip and smacked the glass down. Who cared if the sticky liquid sloshed onto the bar? Krissy had advised her to be rude. She waved to the bartender to bring her another.

"Zoe! There she is! Zoe, is it true your marriage is already over?"

"Did Liam cheat on you?" A harsh voice bellowed over her shoulder.

A blaze of anger flashed through her system. Damn piranhas. But they were making it easy on her. She hadn't had to do a single thing but sit alone at the bar. No scene needed.

Show time.

She tossed back the rest of her margarita and swiveled to face them. She held up one finger. "One question at a time." She added a slight slur to her voice.

A scrawny bald guy scrambled forward with his microphone. "Is it true you left Liam?"

She closed her eyes for a moment and gathered her

energy. She could pull this off. "It's true. Our marriage was a mistake."

A stocky guy with a Weezer baseball cap shouted out the next question. "Did 'Love 'em and Leave 'em Liam' cheat on you?"

Her nostrils flared. Jerk. "You're joking, right? Who would cheat on this?" She waved her hand down her body in the skimpy dress.

"What will happen to the band? Are you leaving?"

The bartender placed her fresh cocktail next to her elbow. She turned away from the pack or reporters and chugged some more tequila before responding.

"Of course not. We've recorded the album. Which is incredible by the way. We're professionals. I'm going to keep partying and doing whatever I want and so is he. End of story." She waved one hand again, like she didn't have a care in the world.

"But you were married for less than a month. Was it even real?" The bleach-blonde shark she recognized from Vegas smirked at her.

Figured the woman was front and center for this story.

"Oh, it was real. We had a very, very good time, if you know what I mean." She winked at scrawny guy. "But I'm too young to settle down. I'm ready to go have fun on tour and a husband would cramp my style. If you know what I mean."

At that comment, another flurry of questions erupted. Fortunately, the hotel's security team rushed to her rescue and herded the unruly media from the bar.

In the abrupt calm after the storm, she turned back to the bar. All her energy deserted her, and she sank into the barstool. Well, that was done, anyway.

"Is this seat taken?" A familiar sexy accent murmured from beside her.

She whipped her head to the side and there he stood, in all his blond, beautiful glory. "Liam?"

His long, blunt fingers gripped the back of the stool, and he raised his eyebrows. "Can I sit?"

"Of course. But what are you doing here? Did the press see you?" Butterflies burst into a full dance in her belly and the hairs on the back of her neck stood at attention.

He folded his long, rangy body onto the chair and turned to her. His emerald eyes gleamed and his lips quirked. "Fuck the press. I'm here for you."

"For me?" So now she was a parrot instead of a singer.

He nodded and pulled a sheet of paper out of his back pocket and handed it to her. "Read this."

Her heart galloped in her chest and her fingers trembled as she accepted the paper. "What is it?"

"A song. Read it." His voice was raspy.

"You wrote a song?"

He narrowed his eyes and growled. "Read. The. Song."

Her heartrate accelerated so much it felt like her heart might leap out of her chest. "Okay." She unfolded the sheet and scanned the words. Her cheeks began to burn.

It was a love song. A duet.

TRUE STARS COLLIDE
> *Brightest star in the sky*
> *You woke me from a long sleep*
> *Your unwavering light struck my heart*
> *Awakening a love so deep*
> *A love so true.*

Her eyes filled and she raised her gaze to his. "You wrote this for me?" He loved her?

He caught both of her hands in his. "Zoe, I wrote this song for us. Because from the moment you came into my life, nothing's been the same. I don't care about image or any of that crap. I've never felt this way. I've never said these words to anyone."

She caught her bottom lip between her teeth and held her breath.

"Zoe Hastings, I love you. You're the most incredible woman I've ever met. I trust you. I love you. You're my true North. Will you marry me?"

Tears streamed down her face and laughter bubbled in her throat. "I'm already your wife, silly."

He shrugged. "Let's do it again. This time, we'll pick out the ring because I know that Real Housewives ring isn't you."

She launched herself into his lap and threw her arms around his neck. "Yes, yes, absolutely yes."

He clasped her chin between two fingers. "Aren't you forgetting something?"

"What? I said yes!"

"Zoe." His chest rumbled.

"Oh, you want the words? I love you, Liam Jones. Now kiss me and take me up to my room. I need to get out of this excuse for a dress."

His eyes lit up and he pressed a quick kiss against her lips. "Oh, love, I'll get you out of that dress alright. Just tell me where to go."

He stood, swept her up in his arms, and strode out of the bar toward her room.

And the rest of their lives.

EPILOGUE

*O*ctober,
PNC Arena,
Raleigh, North Carolina

LIAM SHOVED his hair back from his face and exhaled an unsteady breath. He grabbed the bottle of Cristal and two champagne flutes he'd stashed offstage. It was time for Black Velvet Machine's encore, and they were stoking the audience's fever by waiting another minute before returning to the stage.

They closed every show with an acoustic version of *True Stars Collide*, the duet he'd written for Zoe all those months ago. But tonight was special.

They were in Raleigh, Zoe's hometown, and her mom was in the VIP section backstage with all the band's friends and family. Yeah, he'd survived meeting Zoe's mother and even enjoyed the strong, sweet woman who'd created the love of his life. Seeing them together restored a little faith that there were healthy parent/child relationships in the world.

"Let's go, babe. Ready for our song?" Zoe stroked one slender hand down his arm.

His heart tugged in his chest, and he captured her gorgeous mouth in a quick hot kiss.

"Since it's your hometown, let me introduce the song. And I got us something special for it." He gestured with the bottle toward the stage. "Let's do it, darling."

"I like your style. Follow me." She grinned and sauntered out to the deafening applause of the arena.

The arena was dark except for the spotlight on him and Zoe.

Liam raised the bottle overhead and called out, "You having a good time tonight, Raleigh?"

Cheers and screams greeted them, and he waited until they quieted.

He gazed down at Zoe, drinking in her smiling face and vibrating energy. "So if you all have been around a while, you know I'm not much of a singer. Back-up vocals, yeah, but a duet or a lead? Nah."

"We love you anyway!" A rabid fan screamed from the front row.

Liam's lips quirked. "Thank you. I promise not to sing much. Except for this song. Last summer, when I met this talented woman right here, my entire life transformed. I wasn't one of those blokes who believed in soul mates or any of that love stuff.

"I wrote this duet because Zoe is the perfect woman for me. She's my North Star. She's the strongest, most authentic person I've ever met. Not to mention an incredible singer and rockstar, and gorgeous inside and out. I don't know how I got so lucky for her to choose a jerk like me but I'm not stupid so I'm never letting her go. Will you toast to forever with us?"

He popped the champagne cork and the audience cheered. Zoe stepped into his arms, her golden eyes glistening with tears. "I love you," she whispered and accepted the overflowing glass of champagne.

"You ready?"

Affirmative cheers and applause filled the concert venue. He tossed back his champagne, threw the empty glass over his shoulder, and strummed the opening chords on his guitar. Zoe followed suit, then stepped in closer to him, the lights gleaming off her shiny blue-black hair. With one hand on his shoulder, she began to sing.

Together, they nailed the duet and exited the stage in a cloud of exhilaration and applause.

ZOE FLOPPED into the back of the limo and waited for Liam to join her. Who knew her husband had such a romantic streak? Declaring they were soul mates to twenty-thousand screaming fans. With her mom watching? Her mom and Liam had instantly bonded. She hugged her arms around her waist and savored her happiness.

He slid in next to her and yanked the door closed.

"Where's everyone else? And isn't my mom riding with us to the after-party?"

They'd planned a small late-supper celebration for the band and a few guests at the hotel's penthouse suite.

"She's with the guys and the rest of the crew in the other limo. I wanted a few minutes alone with my beautiful wife."

"Oh really? How long do we have?" She scooted closer to him and wound her arms around his neck. Over the last months, her appetite for him only continued to grow, just like her love for him.

"Not that long, love." He pressed a chaste kiss to the tip of her nose, dropped to one knee, and gazed up into her eyes.

Her pulse kicked in her veins and her face heated. "Liam?"

"Zoe, like I told the crowd, since the day you strutted into the audition, you blew me away with your incredible voice, with your sunny outlook, with your strength and confidence——you've owned my heart." His emerald eyes gleamed in the dim lights of the limousine.

Her heart took a long slow tumble. "Liam, I——"

"I know we got married in Vegas, but I want to marry you for real. Will you be my partner and lover forever?"

Joy filled her. "Yes, I will marry you for real, Liam Jones. You're the only man I've ever loved, and I will love you forever. Come up here and kiss me." She tugged on his hand.

He resisted, whipped out a small velvet box, flipped open the lid, revealing a rare yellow diamond in a delicate gold setting. "Will you wear the ring I chose for you?"

Her eyes widened. "That's the ring we saw in New York. When did you have the time to buy it?"

"I have my tricks. Is that a yes?"

"Absolutely yes. Liam, I can't believe you did this. I love it so much." She slid off the rock their management team had selected and held out her hand. He slipped the ring on her finger, and it was a perfect fit.

He rejoined her on the smooth leather seat, and she climbed onto his lap. "I love you, Zoe. Now we can really celebrate. Kiss me."

She tugged his leonine head down to hers and lost herself in his powerful arms. If she had her way, they'd spend the rest of their lives celebrating their love.

WHAT'S NEXT?

Thanks so much for reading *True Stars Collide*! If you have a moment to leave a review on your favorite retail site, I'd be so appreciative!

If you haven't read the California Suits series yet, start with *Hotel King*. **Read Hotel King now!**

If you haven't read the Pacific Vista Ranch series, start with Sam and Holt's enemies to lovers romance, *Nobody Else But You.*

ALSO BY CLAIRE MARTI

Pacific Vista Ranch Series

Nobody Else But You

The Very Thought of You

For The Love of You

Wrapped Up with You

The Wonder of You

California Suits Series

Hotel King

Wine Country King

Monterey King

Holiday Queen

Palm Springs King

Romance in Laguna Beach Series

Second Chance in Laguna

At Last in Laguna

Sunset in Laguna

ACKNOWLEDGMENTS

When I wrote *Palm Springs King*, Austin's former bandmate Liam made me smile and I knew I wanted to give him more air time. Or page time. The initial version of *True Stars Collide* appeared in the *Rock My World* anthology. I'm so grateful for The New Romance Cafe Publishing group for organizing such a great collection of rockstar stories.

As always, thanks to my my wonderful beta readers and author friends: Joanna Kelly, Donna Stevens Simonetta, Kay Bennett, Christy Hovland, Katie Baldwin, Kerrigan Byrne, and Katie O'Sullivan—you each help me more than you could imagine. I appreciate your time and opinions.

To my wonderful editor, Lindsey Faber, thank you for helping me expand and polish this story. To Shasta Shaefer—thanks for your excellent proofreading skills.

Last but not least, to Todd for your patience and support. I love you. And, finally to my furry kids: Josie and the pussycats: Lola, Beau, and Daisy thanks for providing me unconditional love.

ABOUT THE AUTHOR

Claire Marti is an award winning and *USA Today* Bestselling author of swoonworthy Contemporary Romance novels set in Southern California, including the California Suits series, the Pacific Vista Ranch series, and the Romance in Laguna Beach series. She lives in San Diego with her husband, silly dog, and three clever cats.

Claire started writing stories as soon as she was old enough to pick up pencil and paper. After graduating from the University of Virginia with a BA in English Literature and French, Claire was sidetracked by other careers, including practicing law, selling software for legal publishers, and managing a non-profit animal rescue for a Hollywood actress.

Finally, Claire followed her heart and now focuses on two of her true passions: writing romance and teaching yoga.

www.ingramcontent.com/pod-product-compliance
Lightning Source LLC
Chambersburg PA
CBHW051857130726
47987CB00002B/869